"A wonderful mother from hell fulfills all our worst nightmares. . . . Carla Tomaso knows all our secrets."
—Mary Wings, author of *She Came in a Flash*

ACCLAIM FOR CARLA TOMASO'S FIRST NOVEL *THE HOUSE OF REAL LOVE*

"If *The House of Real Love* is funny, very funny, it is also passionate, searching and serious."
—*Los Angeles Times*

"If you're seeking a 'politically correct' look at contemporary lesbian issues, don't read this book. Ms. Tomaso spares nothing. . . . This narrator is irreverent and funny. . . . The writer never loses sight of the fact that she's trying to tell a story. This novel encourages the reader to laugh at the absurdities of life we take for granted and push at the edges of what we accept as reality."
—*Bay Windows* (Boston)

"Carla Tomaso has given us a rare commodity in lesbian fiction, a prose style with maturity and substance."
—*Baltimore Gay Paper*

"Tomaso takes an irreverent look at the attitudes and issues that affect lesbian relationships. A true lesbian farce, complete with costumes and mistaken identities and no shortage of ribald humor."
—Nisa Donnelly, author of *The Bar Stories*

CARLA TOMASO is a teacher and writer whose short fiction has appeared in the periodical *Common Lives, Lesbian Lives,* and in the anthologies *Unholy Alliances* and *Voyages Out 1.* She is the author of *The House of True Love,* which is also available in a Plume edition. She and her partner live in Pasadena, California.

CARLA TOMASO
MATRICIDE

A PLUME BOOK

PLUME
Published by the Penguin Group
Penguin Books USA Inc., 375 Hudson Street,
New York, New York 10014, U.S.A.
Penguin Books Ltd, 27 Wrights Lane,
London W8 5TZ, England
Penguin Books Australia Ltd, Ringwood,
Victoria, Australia
Penguin Books Canada Ltd, 10 Alcorn Avenue,
Toronto, Ontario, Canada M4V 3B2
Penguin Books (N.Z.) Ltd, 182–190 Wairau Road,
Auckland 10, New Zealand

Penguin Books Ltd, Registered Offices:
Harmondsworth, Middlesex, England

First published by Plume, an imprint of Dutton Signet,
a division of Penguin Books USA Inc.

First Printing, November, 1994
10 9 8 7 6 5 4 3 2 1

Ⓟ REGISTERED TRADEMARK—MARCA REGISTRADA

LIBRARY OF CONGRESS CATALOGING-IN-PUBLICATION DATA:

Tomaso, Carla.
    Matricide / Carla Tomaso.
      p. cm.
    ISBN 0-425-27111-8
    1. Mothers and daughters—United States—Fiction. 2. Women authors,
American—Psychology—Fiction. 3. Lesbians—United States—Fiction. I. Title.
PS3570.04297M37 1994
813'.54—dc.20   94-6876
                                                                 CIP

Printed in the United States of America
Designed by Leonard Telesca

For Naomi

Acknowledgments

I would like to thank everyone who encouraged
and supported me in writing this book,
especially Mary Hayden, Lyle Steele
and my editor, Carole DeSanti.

1

It was one of those mornings when getting out of bed seemed impossible, even dangerous. All I could think of to do instead of lying there forever was to try to find somebody and fall in love.

Which is pretty tough when you're flat on your back, in bed, alone. Falling in love the last time was another main reason I was in bed now, picking at my cuticles and chain smoking Kents. But why think about that? Just because everything good holds the seeds of everything bad as sure as death comes after birth?

I was also trying to forget this sickening nightmare I'd just had where I'd taken a butcher knife to my very own mother. Her big blue eyes were on me during the whole thing, even when the blade slipped through the artery in her throat pouring blood all over white skin, black hair, yellow carpet. Fellini couldn't have done it better. And although nobody can control their own unconscious, it still made me feel like a shit to be dreaming about putting a knife into my own mother's throat, especially when I hadn't even seen her in ten years.

The phone rang a few minutes later. I let it ring until it stopped because I couldn't think of anybody calling who would make me feel better. Everybody any good, Emily Dickinson, Virginia Woolf, Colette, was already dead. Instead of answering I flicked an ash onto the floor and watched it lie there, gray and stupid. I wanted to go all the way to the bottom fast so at least I'd know where I was and dropping ashes on my own wood floor would be about as close as I'd ever get. I'd never be able to actually grind out a butt there, that much was clear.

Already the smoke in my bedroom was beginning to get on my nerves. The swirling gray clouds were no longer interesting or romantic at all. It was obvious. I wasn't made for being depressed. I wasn't French or had a slow metabolism. In reality, the worst thing about my life right now wasn't murder and it wasn't love. It was that I had the day off work and nobody I wanted to spend it with.

When the phone rang again I answered it.

It wasn't Virginia Woolf. It was Doris.

"Ah," she said. "You are home."

"Yes," I said. "I'm lying around doing nothing." I didn't tell her about the dream. You never know how people feel about murder, even if it's only in your head.

"In bed smoking cigarettes," Doris said.

Doris loved me but only in a certain way. She liked to help me out of my failures because life was like a fix-it game to her, the same reason people become electricians or hairdressers or plumbers.

"Exactly," I said. I wasn't surprised. Doris knew most things about me, no matter how much I hid them. Her last idea for my life had been that I was going to design expensive silver goddess jewelry for Tiffany's.

"Like Paloma Picasso," she'd said, "except you tell them the shapes are breasts and uteruses and vaginal canals. Forget abstraction. *The Wall Street Journal* just said that feminism as a marketing concept has finally reached upscale shoppers."

"You do it, Doris," I'd said then like I always did.

"You're the talented one," she'd said as usual. "I just read trends."

"It's my day off," I said now. "You gave it to me, remember?"

"You ought to be outside doing something healthy," she said. "Not lying in bed feeling sorry for yourself."

It wasn't that I'd ever made jewelry or had an artistic sense at all. I was a high school English teacher and Doris was my boss.

We'd discovered feminism together a few years before and since then I was the person who was supposed to live out her ambitions.

"I made a mistake when I woke up," I said.

"What?" she said.

"I started thinking about my life."

"That's just what I was calling about," she said.

"Give me a break, Doris," I said. "I'm suicidal. I'm putting ashes on my own floor."

"Shut up and listen," she said, but she wasn't being mean. That's just the way she talks.

"I was flipping through *Women's Directions* when I came upon an announcement for a summer writers' conference. For women only," she said.

"Rip-off," I said. "Bunch of burned-out writers looking for a fast buck and an easy lay." I'd been to a writers' conference fifteen years before when I'd had aspirations of my own. I'd watched a bearded alcoholic adventure novelist screw a different young girl hopeful every night of the week. During the day, he popped Valium for his hangover and made hostile comments to the rest of us about the puerility of our manuscripts.

"But all-women," Doris said as if that made a difference.

"So you saw this announcement and you thought of me," I said. "Why?" I was always interested in what Doris said about her choices for my life. It told what she thought about my character and my gifts even though she was mostly talking about herself.

"I think you should try again," she said, meaning being a writer. "This time, though, I think you ought to try poetry. Its spareness and subtlety fit you better now."

"Why?" I said.

"You've had a very stimulating life so far," she went on. "And you're extremely sensitive about what things look like and what people say." Doris thinks everybody else is sensitive because life to her is such a straight shot.

"Doris," I said, "nobody has ever encouraged me to be a writer, much less a poet. Not the astrologer, not my career counselor, not my own high school English teacher to whom I wrote

Elizabethan and Italian sonnet sequences often ending in couplets like this:

> "And if you do remember me be fair,
> For you are all I know of life or care."

"And that was only in high school," Doris said.

"Magazine editors, publishers, agents, other writers, no one encouraged me, Doris," I said. "Do you get the picture?"

"Hmm," she said, busy with something else already.

"Listen," I said, "thanks for thinking of me but I guess I'll just stay in bed and dwell on how pointless and empty it all is."

"What's it?" Doris said. "You've got a fine life."

"That's not the point," I said.

"Maybe you'll meet some nice people at this conference," she said then, which, I realized, was her code way of telling me that maybe I'd find a girlfriend there. One who would last.

Many years ago, before I knew what it meant to be a lesbian, I'd written my only work of fiction, a bad novel about love. The five main characters were all women in love with somebody. The only happy one was the lesbian character who had found a woman who cared about her and loved her with honesty, depth and passion. I described the two of them in flowery, earnest prose doing things like cooking complicated meals, trekking in Nepal and marching hand in hand for lesbian rights. I know better now. I knew I couldn't write fiction and I knew lesbian love wasn't like that. No matter what anybody said.

2

A few cigarettes after I hung up with Doris I decided to get up.
The sheets and the smoke were beginning to bum me out and
the cats had started to take turns jumping on my stomach and
walking across my face.

My lovers, when each one moved out, kept leaving their cats
behind. The cats would curl up around each other and clean
each other's foreheads and tails while the woman who I thought
was my true soul mate at last was walking out the door with my
suede jacket or my portable disk player safely packed in her suitcase. Right alongside my bloody, broken heart.

"Bye, honey," the last one had said a few months ago. "I know
you meant well. Keep the cat. She's happy here."

This morning I went downstairs to the kitchen with the cats
brushing my ankles, trying to shepherd me toward their food. I
was toying with the crazy idea that maybe the cats had each
taken on the personality of their former owner.

"Okay, Jenny," I said to the orange one while spooning out
some tuna.

"Here you go, Kate," I said to the gray while she lapped up
her cream.

Amanda was sitting off by herself near the sink pretending not
to be hungry. I called her name and clicked my tongue to show

her she was special and she padded over to me, slinky and seductive as hell.

I usually try to blame the right person for my unhappiness. Today, the ex-girlfriends, Doris, my coworkers, even my long-lost mother, seemed strangely benign. So while I was changing the three boxes of cat litter I keep by the back door I read the paper I was using for lining as if some message about what to do to feel better was going to jump out at me from the newsprint. And indeed, looking up from Part Two, Events of Interest to Women, was a big picture of what's-her-name, the famous poet, confrontational and older than I remembered from the reading I'd attended several years before.

She was this year's attraction for the writers' conference Doris had mentioned on the phone. And she wasn't a bad one at that. Before she came out as a lesbian, her books of poetry had won all sorts of national and international awards.

I pulled the paper out from under Mandy who was getting ready to pee. The conference was going to be in Taos. The famous poet's name was Blaire Bennett. There was mention of Mabel Dodge Luhan and D. H. Lawrence and a vaguely erotic reference to the anthropomorphic desert landscape. I thought about men in love and women in love and everybody in love with themselves and nature and snakes and bear rugs.

When that last girlfriend left she'd also said, "You were so good for me. You helped me get in touch with my repressed memories, the flashbacks, my true sexuality. Now I'll finally be able to share myself intimately with another human being. You saved my life, literally." Then she'd sashayed out the front door in tight jeans and high-heeled boots ready to take on everything in the world except me.

Last night she called to tell me she was doing fine. They always want to make sure you know that, that they're working their steps, meeting great people, facing life with eyes open wide. The phone call was another big reason I was such a mess today. I couldn't think of anything in my life to say back.

"I know, I know," Doris said to me one hot night a few weeks later when she opened the gate to her house. "I've already hired a new gardener. The old one just stopped showing up. Can you imagine letting all these plants die?"

I'd spent the first part of the summer alternately writing poems to submit to the writers' conference and trying to talk Doris into going at all. Doris was smart so that wasn't the problem, it was just that basically all she wanted to do in life was give up and die. Sure, I had major intimacy problems, but Doris was way beyond me. She didn't give a shit about anything at all.

I did. All of a sudden this writers' conference was giving meaning to my life, not that I had any literary hopes or fictional aspirations. But, it had helped me decide to try something new about solving my love thing. I was going to cultivate deep and lasting friendships with Doris and the other conference participants. I was going to forget about sex and learn to distill and sublimate my feelings into small, perfectly faceted gems of verse. As clear as a teardrop, as complex as a flake of snow, each line would be about the experience, so maybe I could take a break from living it out.

"The gardener probably thought you'd at least water them," I said. "They're your plants."

"Take some lemons home with you, please," Doris said.

"Okay," I said. Then I put one up to my nose and sniffed.

Another good thing was that in the past few weeks, while I was so busy writing bad poems, I hadn't had any more killer nightmares about my mother, at least any that I could remember. So I was pretty optimistic about that too. That maybe I could begin to get a full night's sleep for a change.

"You ever dream about your parents?" I asked Doris.

"Want a drink?" she said. We sat down in the patio by the lemon tree even though everything looked like hell. The plastic deck chairs weren't all that clean either.

"Your mom or your dad?" I said.

"No," Doris said. "I never dream a thing. My nights are as black and boring as death."

"You just don't remember," I said.

"Probably," Doris said. She wasn't interested in this at all. She wanted to get us our drinks more than anything.

I often wondered why I cared about Doris given what a deadbeat she was. It could have been some sort of parent fixation or maybe a Pygmalion fetish. Whatever it was it didn't bear much examination. I just wanted her to be better. But I didn't have a clue about the magical thing that was going to make her love life again. And she was beginning to drink. A lot.

She was sixty now and she always said she'd had three lives: fourteen years as a nun, fourteen years as a wife and now, fourteen years as a widow/principal of a girls' high school. Technically she hadn't been a nun for quite all the fourteen years, but she counted from the time she first got the idea.

"We won't notice the weeds when it gets dark," she said with a laugh when she handed me my drink.

"We won't be able to see each other either," I said.

Doris lit a cigarette and then handed me a piece of cocktail pumpernickel with Brie on it. "So if I go to this conference with you do I have to write something too?" she said.

"Oh, shut up," I said.

"Excuse me," she said, like maybe her hearing was starting to go.

"I just don't feel like dragging you through this experience,

Doris. I want you to do it on your own." I knew for a fact that she could write pure gold when she wanted to. "You're the one who wanted to go to this conference in the first place," I said. "Admit it." I was making emphatic motions with my glass and wine was sloshing down my wrist and onto the deck. We both watched the dark spots there until they dried.

"You could probably reinvent the language at your little telephone desk while you wait for your steak to broil," I said softly. "You probably have a novel hidden under your bed that's more genius than James Joyce."

"Did you bring your poems?" she said.

"I'm on to you, Doris. You're trying to throw me off the scent." I wasn't usually this hard on her but since my recent decision to be into intense friendship I couldn't seem to let anything slide.

"Want another drink?" she said, standing up.

By the time Doris came back I had five lemons to take home with me in a nice row on the table between us. I'd also forgiven her even though her worst problems weren't entirely her own fault. Whose were?

"So let's write something," I said. "For our applications."

"Now?" she said.

"Sure," I said. "And then we can read out loud to each other."

"Swell," she said. I couldn't believe it. "I'll get the paper. What shall we write about first? Childhood incest memories, adolescent identity crises, the 'first time'? How about a poem dealing with shameful masturbatory fantasies?" And then she pretended to read aloud.

> "I like bondage, I like groups,
> Put me in a cage and call in the troops."

She smiled through the dusk. Her eyes scared me but I was damned if I'd let her get to me so easy.

"That's a ditty, Doris, not a poem. Are you going to be serious or shall I just go home?" I lobbed one of my lemons at her and it landed in her lap. She left it there, nesting, to annoy me.

"What a crab," she said. "No wonder you can't find a girl-friend who will stick around for more than a week or two."

That was meaner than Doris usually is so I knew I was definitely getting to her. When she stood up to get another drink I figured what the hell? You try to be a friend to people and you have to say things that matter. Otherwise, what difference does it make?

"Kind of hitting the bottle hard lately, aren't you, Doris?"

She looked at me fast. I'd never before mentioned her drinking except as a joke. I'd just leaped a boundary high enough to take anybody's breath away.

"Go home," she said and then she went inside the house and slammed the door at me.

What did I do? I stayed right there and felt friendless as hell. And single too, of course. Who was I kidding? So maybe Doris took care of things through booze. All I did different was that I filled up on bad girlfriends. And now it was getting even worse. I was beginning to doubt if I could do any kind of human relationships at all.

I thought about all the couples living all over those canyon hills getting on each other's nerves right now but also feeling really safe, like being in a couple meant there was a net under whatever your personal high-wire act happened to be. I got so sad I was actually considering knocking on Doris's door and telling her I wanted to get drunk with her. I mean how could I stand to be sober and think about how I was never even casually held anymore or how I never had anybody to listen to my boring dreams in the morning?

Then I realized something even sadder. How none of my lovers who lived with me had actually taken care of me when I was sick or ever even held me in a satisfying way. How I'd never remotely made love like you're supposed to where you feel as one with your partner, for example, and how I'd never loved a girlfriend enough to want to have a child with her.

I had to face it. The love I'd felt was always exciting, at least in the beginning, but it was never deep. Never as deep as it was in my dreams. How being in a couple didn't make anything any better for me. I sighed and rubbed my eyes. But just before I threw myself totally into serious and consuming self-pity, Doris came back outside.

I'm not sure that she hadn't just made a mistake and figured I'd left by now but I gave her the benefit of the doubt because I was so lonely. Maybe she knew I was still here and wanted to make up.

"Hi, Doris," I said softly because it was dark now and I didn't want to scare her.

"Aren't you cold?" she said.

"Not really," I said. "But I'd better be going." And then I stood up.

"What about dinner?" she said.

"What about it?" I said.

"It's all served up and on the table," she said. And then she said real formally, "And I'd like you to join me."

So we were friends again and, even though it goes against all the intervention books, I conspired with her not to talk about anything hard for at least the entire meal.

My First Poem

Silence

A dinner party
Ends.
The guests are staring
At each other,
Still chewing.

You write a letter.
The handwriting
Rises
A little more
With each new line.

Driving north on
Highway One
You imagine
Yourself

Turning the wheel
Sharply to the
Left
And flying
At last.

4

My car was the only cool thing I owned. That's what the kids at school told me. Not that they knew what else I owned. They were only making an educated guess.

I liked to drive fast at night next to the ocean with the top down. It was pure cinematic crap but that was also the point. Driving fast gave me the illusion of power and purpose. I pretended I was on the road to somewhere hot, having a fabulous time getting there, too.

Many of my ex-lovers wanted me initially for my car. Of course, nobody ever said that but you could see it in their eyes. They didn't look at me when we were standing near it. They looked at it. Subconsciously they were trying to make me be my car, sleek and strong and self-assured. I could tell what they were doing and I let them do it anyway. I just pretended to be a certain kind of boy.

It was okay with me to have a cool car. After all, it took nerve to believe I could handle such a tough machine and that was cool too. And if I wasn't exactly the same as my car, if that was a gradual disappointment to some people, well, whose fault was that?

Today I was on my way somewhere for real. I was going to the writers' conference in Taos by way of Doris's house to pick her up. And I still had to stop for Cokes at the liquor store and sandwiches at the deli but I wasn't in any hurry. Doris and I had decided that the point of the conference was all the great stuff we were going to see along the way.

At least that's what we decided out loud.

Privately I was making Doris go to get her off her ass. And I was going to get a different angle on my life. Probably I'd been looking at things from too close to home.

I had to sit outside the liquor store for a few minutes until it opened. It was a cold, gray morning. Odd for July in LA but a good omen too because Taos was going to seem farther away than ever, in a new climate zone, so to speak.

"Hi, Teach." I looked up to see Tina jumping over the door into the passenger seat, like she'd practiced it for hours in P.E.

"Hi, Tina," I said, as cool as my car. "What's up?"

"I'm ditching my summer job," Tina said. "I just now decided. It's meaningless and exploitive and it's draining my soul."

"Welcome to the real world," I said and immediately wished I hadn't.

"It's like you said in class last year," she said, fiddling with the push buttons on the car radio. "About being an adult was by definition about being a hypocrite."

I remembered that. It was one of my better classes. Tina and the rest of the seniors had just read *Antigone* and *The Catcher in the Rye* and what I'd actually said was they'd all be hypocrites by the time they got to be adults. It worked. They were pissed.

"No way," Monica Valencia had said.

"Just look at the adults around you," I said. "They are all hypocrites. They can't help it."

There was a moment of total silence while they thought about it. They couldn't quite decide.

"I can see that you need an example," I'd said. "I'll prove my point in half a minute. When you're adults you'll drive by homeless people every day on your way to work and then you'll go home at night and curl up in front of your fat audiovisual unit to watch *Lifestyles of the Rich and Famous*. And on Sunday, you'll go to Mass and pray for the poor and less fortunate. Won't you?"

"I won't watch *Lifestyles of the Rich and Famous*," said Julie Perry.

"That's not the point, you jerk," said Tina, who always seemed to know exactly what the point was. "To not be a hypocrite when you grow up you have to either be a saint or kill yourself," she said.

Then everybody looked so unhappy that I tried to change the subject. That's the way it is with teaching high school. You have to keep breaking kids of their youthful idealism but only a little bit at a time. Like: "Not all governments tell the truth," one week and "Not all adults are grown-ups" the next. A month later maybe "Many people destroy each other because of love." It was too mean to do it all at once.

Tina had graduated in June and now it was July which meant that our relationship had undergone some changes, one of which was evidenced by her use of the word "Teach." She'd really wanted to use my first name but she didn't quite dare. That would come in September at the alumnae banquet.

And it was also clear that Tina wanted to talk about her life. She wasn't moving. She was looking straight ahead.

"You need me to drive you somewhere, Tina?" I asked her. "I'm pretty much on my way to take a vacation now."

But it was like she hadn't heard me.

I was absolutely not the kind of teacher who encouraged student disclosures. Once in a while they tried to tell me about a bad boyfriend or parents and I looked at them so blankly that they usually excused themselves right in the middle and left. But now I was really trapped. And even worse, I was sort of interested in what Tina had to say.

"I got laid last night," she said, finally.

"Uh-huh," I said. And suddenly this wasn't that much fun anymore.

"For the first time," she said.

"Oh well," I said lamely, "that happens. High school graduation and all. Transitions. Growing up and all. We reach out to boyfriends for comfort and stability." I was wanting a cigarette badly now and I was hoping that I was sounding so pedantic that Tina would hop out of the passenger seat and skip along home.

"We," she said sarcastically, "got laid by our girlfriend. We hadn't ever done that before. We're pretty freaked out."

"Oh," I said. "I'm sorry."

"Don't be sorry," Tina said. "I just need somebody to talk to so I can come back down to earth. I was taking a walk and thinking how much I'd like to talk to you and then here was your cool car parked right here."

"It was like a sign, huh?" I said and then I had déjà vu for no reason at all. Maybe there was something familiar in the absolute strangeness of the moment.

Tina was looking at me wistfully, like I was still her teacher and any minute now things were going to make sense.

"There was something about the way you taught *The Color Purple* and that May Sarton novel right in a row that made me think you'd understand," she said.

"So how do you feel about the experience?" I said.

"Kind of permeable," Tina said. "Like suddenly I'm part of the human continuum. Like we're all one or something."

"Uh-huh," I said.

"But, kind of sad at the same time, like we're all just so separate, too." Poor Tina was beginning to cry. I didn't think I could stand it.

"Do you have to cry?" I said.

"What?" she said.

"Do you have to cry?"

"I guess not," she said, wiping her nose on her sleeve. "I guess I can stop. You want me to leave?"

"No," I said. "It's good you're talking to me. It's just the crying."

"Okay," she said. And then she breathed in and out for a little while. "It's not so much that it's a girl I did it with. It's more that I did it."

Two things to think about at the same time. That's how it had been with me, exactly. Except that I had been older when it happened and more guilty and without anybody to talk to. Tina was lucky. She had me.

I looked at the side of her head. She had thick, straight blond hair that hung down to her jawbone and two silver studs in her left earlobe. She knew a lot for an eighteen-year-old but she was also making things more difficult than she had ever imagined.

Unless things were easier for lesbians now. Unless women had gotten nice.

"Go on," I said, gently, hoping she wouldn't.

She didn't say anything for a long time and I began to get nervous. Of course, Doris knew I was a lesbian and so did everybody else at work no doubt but they never mentioned it to me. Now here was Tina about to come out for both of us and I wasn't going to be able to hide behind May Sarton's literary slacks like I did in class.

"You don't actually know her," Tina said. "She's in my youth group at church. We had a girls' overnight at the retreat camp in the mountains. We shared a tent. And then, well, you know."

"Oh?" I said.

"Aren't you a lesbian?" Tina said then, inevitably. "I was always under that impression. I mean, correct me if I'm wrong."

"It's more complicated than that," I said, while thinking just the opposite. The truth may be uncomfortable but it's always as simple as snow. "I've loved many people in my life," I went on. "Some of them men, some of them women." I hated myself. Tina should have hated me too.

But she didn't. She did this big thing. She reached over and took my hand in hers. I lost my breath. I couldn't see a thing out of the windshield of my car.

"Oh hell," I said.

"It's okay," Tina said. "It's okay."

I might as well have been stark naked. At least I wasn't crying.

"I understand," she said.

"Oh, shut up," I said. But we kept holding hands anyway, even when a bunch of construction workers walked right past the car to buy sandwiches in the liquor store.

"I have to tell you about last night," she said, finally. "I promise not to cry but I have to tell somebody or it's too weird."

"I have to go pick up Doris for our vacation," I said.

"Doris Hamilton, the principal?" Tina said. "Are you two lovers? Oh my God."

"No," I said. "She's not a lesbian. We're going to a writers' conference in New Mexico for the hell of it."

"Can I go?" Tina said.

And because I was certain she was kidding, I said, "Sure."

My poem #2

Oral Geography

A dark cave of secret, hidden things
Gold, silver and porcelain
And words
Formed by the tongue and lips
But dead.
Inhaled before
Anyone can hear them.
And decay,
Invisible,
Sweet smelling rot,
Gray,
Silent,
Remote as the moon.
Until one day,
A crack, a split,
As you chew a pecan.
Or half a tooth comes out
In your hand,
Embedded in a piece of
Saltwater taffy
Like a pearl.
Or nothing happens at all
Until one night,
After a party,
Or after love,
You wake up
Screaming.

Doris didn't submit poetry to the conference. She submitted a
series of successful and moving speeches she'd already delivered
to parents' groups, baccalaureates, graduations, report card

nights. The anonymous selection committee loved her work and wanted her, wanted her, wanted her. Me they wanted too but not nearly so unreservedly. I was accepted into the morning poetry workshop where we were taught the basics of prosody so we could practice technique in the afternoon. The real poets got to be in the afternoon seminar where they could critique each other's poems with sensitive yet brutal honesty.

I felt like a fool. Or Doris's chaperon. And if Tina came along who was going to sit in the backseat?

5

"I'm serious," Tina said.

"I'm not," I said. "And besides me, you've got to know what Doris Hamilton would think of the idea."

"She doesn't even like kids," Tina said.

"Exactly," I said. "Plus I barely got her to agree to come with me in the first place. She'd never go if you did."

I was actually kind of proud of Doris for being such a hard-ass. She never played around at work with being sweet or soft. Once I bought her a button that read "I am not your mother" which she wore to school for one week straight. Everybody seemed to finally get the point.

"I'll handle it," Tina said.

"It costs money; they probably don't take teens; you'd have to quit your job; I won't take responsibility; your parents will never let you," I said.

"I said I'd handle it," Tina said and she hopped out of the car. "I'll call Dr. Hamilton and explain and then I'll run home and deal with my parents. It's going to be hot there, right? Oh, and give me the number of the conference organizers so I can clear things with them too, okay?"

I handed her the brochure.

"I'll be back in half an hour," she said. "I live right around the corner. Oh"—she turned back to me—"you want a Coke or a magazine or something to pass the time?" She waved at the liquor store. "This is awfully nice of you. It kind of saves my life."

"But I don't want you to come," I shouted.

"Yes you do." Tina smiled.

"Why do I?" I said.

"Because I remind you of you," she said, "twenty years ago." And then she ran off down the street.

I sat in my car and smoked a cigarette, feeling rather pleasantly out of control. Tina was going to handle things, a job for which she had much more energy than I did. Some people might suggest that I was the adult and therefore should have taken charge but that kind of logic didn't stir me at all. I was no longer her teacher and, besides, it goes without saying that a capacity for grown-up behavior has nothing to do with chronological age at all.

But she was dead wrong about reminding me of me. It was a terrific line but it was half-baked. I had nowhere near Tina's life force when I was eighteen. At eighteen I was afraid of almost everything including cold weather, other people and myself. I was certain that, at any given moment, everyone was snickering at me, waiting for me to slip on the ice. Tina probably loved to skate.

The selection committee member who answered Tina's phone call thought it charming that she wanted to come along with us. Student, principal and teacher. They could photograph and interview us and use the story for their next brochure. To sort of lend a straight, middle-of-the-road angle to the Women Only concept. Why else would she offer Tina a half scholarship and waive the submission requirement?

And her parents. Well, what better company could they ask for their daughter than teacher and principal? Her mother, a slender woman with a ponytail who looked younger than me, drove Tina back to my car and loaded the suitcase into the truck. She handed me a tin of Toll House cookies and a $50 bill for gas.

"Is this really okay with you?" she said.

"Sure," I said. Was that too strange? Did she think I was a bloodless spinster schoolteacher with nothing better to do than hang out with teenagers all summer? Or worse, did she wonder if I was a lecherous dyke with designs on her girl?

"Tina showed me the brochure and I spoke with the person in charge so I guess everything's squared away," she said. "I kind of wish I was going too. It sounds great. But I can't write at all."

"Me neither," I said. "I'm in a beginner's workshop about po-etry." Tina hopped into the backseat and began pulling equip-ment out of her pack—visor, sunscreen, magazine, Walkman. I wondered what it was like to have a nice, normal mother who seemed to be fully human. Did it make you write better poetry or worse?

"Tina really admired you as a teacher," her mother said. "She learned so much about life from you. She was always bringing up your name."

I loved it. She could have gone on like this all morning and I wouldn't have gotten bored. And I never doubted her sincerity. When do you ever doubt the honesty of somebody who's flatter-ing you?

But it was time to go. Mom patted me on the hand. "Have fun," she said. I pulled out into the traffic and she waved and waved at us, just like in the movies.

"Nice mom," I shouted to Tina, over my shoulder.

"Yeah," was all Tina said. Maybe it was boring to have too good of a mother. I'd never thought of that. "Doris Hamilton wasn't pleased about my joining you," she said. "She's the only glitch in the plans. I told her I'd split at any time. I'd just jump out of the car and take the bus home. I swore to that."

"She's not mad at you," I said. "She's mad at me."

"Obviously," Tina said.

We were getting on the freeway now to go to Doris's house so it was too noisy to talk. I wanted to know if Tina had told the girl she'd just slept with that we were leaving and if we got to discuss it in front of Doris. I sort of hoped that maybe one of us had somebody to love.

After about ten minutes we got off the freeway. Tina was busy reading a book. When we got to her house Doris put her suitcase in the trunk and then got into the front seat. Everybody smiled strongly and said "hi." The whole thing was beginning to feel like a very bad mistake.

6

The story of my life until now was about two things: driving my
mother and me into a tree on purpose ten years ago and getting
left by all the women I thought I loved. I'd never told anybody
about the first thing because who wanted to hear about stuff like
that? The car crash was scary; it was ugly and it was damned embarrassing. Mostly I tried to forget it had happened at all. The
second thing was harder. It wasn't so easy to forget about getting
left by your lover over and over and over.

Today, I was setting out on what I hoped was the beginning of
the third thing: the deep and lasting friendship thing.

One of the big motivators for friendship was that here I was
supposed to be a lesbian feminist and my relationships were ending just like in all the heterosexual love movies. On the screen,
it's supposed to break your heart when somebody walks out but
in truth you don't give a damn because neither person in the
couple has a clue what the other one is like anyway. I hated to
admit it but all my broken relationships were just as stupid as
that. I might as well have been straight.

Just past a "Last Gas for 45 Miles" sign two or three hours into
the trip, I decided to be celibate. Like Doris except with me it'd
be on purpose. I'd practice peaceful self-involvement and intense friendships until I was good and ready for love.

I could still see the road perfectly well but behind my eyes things were getting hazy with wishful thinking. When I fell in love again I'd go all the way and be completely open and honest and real like I'd never been before. I'd make big love with my eyes open wide. I'd be able to love like we were one person and then happily separate to be two. I also figured that I kind of had to hurry because I was already forty-one years old.

After we got gas nobody told me to put the top up even though it had to be a hundred and twenty degrees on the road. Both girls looked happy to me. Doris was smoking now and watching the yucca go by and Tina was writing as fast as she could. She was evidently too young to be wary and paralyzed from the weight of failed ambition like Doris and I were.

"Name some cold things," Tina said, leaning forward from the backseat. "Want to use my spray bottle? I filled it with water before we left."

"Sure," Doris said. She took the bottle and sprayed her round face and double chin. She sprayed her flabby, fat upper arms like she had no shame at all, like that excess skin was all the same to her. "You want some?" she said to me. "I'll spray you." I nodded so she sprayed me too.

"Cold things," Tina said. "I need some cold things."

"I've seen kids carry these bottles around at school but I never knew what they were for," Doris said, like she was real excited about it. Then she sprayed the back of her neck.

"Ice cubes," I said.

"Complete silence," Doris said. "When you finally realize that somebody is dead."

"Wow," Tina said.

I said, "Walking into the Pacific Ocean on a day like this. On a day when the beach burns your feet."

"Buying time," Doris said.

"The sound of leaves crackling behind you when you're walking in the dark." Nobody responded. "It's hard to do this when you're driving," I said.

"After making love when you can't think of anything to say," Tina said. "I wrote a poem just now, about it. Want to hear it?"

"Sure," Doris said, of course. Who wouldn't? Especially Doris who, in spite of her job description, probably hadn't been with a teenager this long in forty years.

Teens have the reputation of being erratic, emotionally demanding and basically a drag but that wasn't the case as far as I could tell. Mostly I'd found they had a nice combination of innocence and experience; they were smart and not all that cynical yet. They were us adults sliced thin.

Tina's Poem

Sex

I want to have a daughter of my own
When I grow up.
She doesn't even have to look like me.
I'll love her anyway.

"That's a good beginning," I said. "That captures my imagination."

"Ssh," Doris said, self-righteous as hell. "You're not her teacher anymore." It was obvious that Doris knew nothing about anything, least of all teaching. When you were somebody's teacher, you're always their teacher in spite of everybody's intentions to the contrary.

"Go on," Doris said.

But once she grows up
Or when she's growing up
She won't find out about sex from me.

She can ask her friends.
She can study positions
In magazines
At the sleazy newsstand.
But if she asks me about it
I won't say a thing.
I'll just take her in my arms and rock her.
Like my baby,
Who never had to grow up.

"Well, it made me think," Doris said, after a moment. "But you have to explain to me what the big thing is about sex."

"That's easy," Tina said. "It's because everybody wants to be close to somebody and they think sex is how you do it." I wondered why everything only gets more complicated as you get older. To think that Tina could explain sex in one compound sentence. "That's partly what the poem is about," she said.

"We'll probably be in the same poetry workshop," I said to Tina, "at the writers' conference." It was a depressing thought but I tried not to let it show.

"You want me to drive now?" Tina said.

"Can I trust you with my cool car?" I said. I was semi-serious although I was the only one here with a near fatality on my driving record. I pulled us over at a treeless rest stop where everything was gravel and struggling oleander bushes irrigated by drip hoses at night. Doris went off to the bathroom.

"You have to call that girl," I said to Tina, "from your church group?"

"No," she said. "We hardly know each other. You probably really loved the first person you were with." We were sitting on top of a wooden picnic table under a concrete shelter. There were a lot of big recreational vehicles and retired people and little kids around. Nobody like us.

"Not exactly," I said. "It might be better not to. There's plenty to think about without that."

Then Doris came back and Tina went to the bathroom.

"You going to sit in the backseat now?" Doris said to me.

"You've got toilet tissue on your shoe," I said.

"This is not my idea of a vacation," she said. She sat down next to me on top of the picnic table. "And what's with Tina?"

"Nothing," I said. "She just had sex for the first time."

"Oh," she said.

"With a girl," I said. It wasn't mine to tell but for some reason I felt better after telling it.

"Wonderful," Doris said, like I'd just told her Tina was pregnant or dying of something. Maybe she felt left out because of being the only one who hadn't been with a woman.

"Admit it," I said, putting an arm around her soft shoulders, "you're having a good time."

"I hope a low flying bird shits on your head," she said.

7

I could tell that Tina wanted to drive fast, but she didn't speed.
There was all this rippling held-back energy across her neck and
back and in the way she kept us just under the speed limit and
tried not to tailgate. She also didn't play the radio. She and I
and Doris were each twenty years apart which is a big deal when
you're considering areas like music and speed. So I appreciated
Tina's self-control. In other ways, age was turning out to mean
hardly anything at all.

After half an hour or so of nothing happening I decided to
read my poem about sex back at Tina.

My poem #3

Sex

Outside the bedroom
The film crew sat, smoking,
Playing cards.

One guy, an old gray bearded type,
Slapped down an Ace of Spades.
"I win," he said, again.

One girl, a young poetic type,
Filed her nails and thought

About her last vacation
And her next.

From the bedroom, a huge sigh.
"Ah," the gray guy said.
"Finally," the girl said.

"Some people take fucking forever,"
She said.
"Even when nobody's watching,"
He said.
"Somebody's always watching,"
She said.
"Come on," he said.
"I'll buy you lunch."

"I think that's excellent," Tina said, taking her eyes off the road for only a second or two to look at me. "Although I'm not sure I exactly understand it. The idea may take more life experience than I've actually had."

"Life experience doesn't help at all in understanding sex," Doris said, which pissed me off, partly because it hurt my pride and partly because I wanted her to be wrong. "It works just the opposite, come to think of it."

Right now I was looking at both of us through the eyes of Tina. Here I was with my weird existential poem about lovemaking and here was Doris waxing cynical in a particularly unattractive way. I wanted to give Tina something to look forward to.

"We're probably not typical," I said.

"Oh, I know that," Tina said.

By the time we got to Taos, I was so tired of Doris and Tina that I had begun to actually hate the back of their heads, the way Tina's blond hair was cut straight across the top of her shoulders like she was some Hitler youth on exchange and Doris's thick pugilist's neck was shaved and stubbly up to where her regular hair hit. At least they liked each other.

To hell with friendship was what I was thinking now. I was almost back to wanting to fall in love again no matter how much it hurt. No matter how empty and meaningless it turned out to be.

"We're here," Tina said all of a sudden. And we were. We were at the gate of El Encanto, a low adobe arch and two tall wooden doors with silver studs hammered in a pattern that spelled PEACE across the top.

Doris took out the conference brochure from her notebook and began to read to us. "The conference will be held at the estate of the late Paul Jenkins, heir to the Jenkins beer fortune, sponsor of writers and painters, ex-priest, ex-Buddhist monk, ex-stockbroker. Dorothy Jenkins, his daughter, has generously opened the estate to our conference for the past ten years. 'I do it because I love women and I love writers,' says Dorothy."

"I wonder if Dorothy's a lesbian," Tina said.

"You know it took me ten years after finding out I was one to be able to say that word," I said. "And here you are at eighteen, 'lesbian' this and 'lesbian' that. 'Is she a lesbian? I'm a lesbian. Are you a lesbian?' "

Doris thought this was so funny she choked on her cigarette.

"What are you laughing at?" I said. "Who are you to laugh? You with your big fat heterosexual privilege strutting behind you like a goddamn bodyguard. Learn some respect for oppression, would you?"

Doris nodded very soberly but her eyes were still a big joke.

"First thing to learn," I said at Tina, "first thing to learn is you can't trust a heterosexual. Not really. Not with anything about your life." I was looking at Tina but I was really talking to Doris. I was so cranky I wanted to get them both at once.

"Things to chat about are okay but straights don't understand shame and they don't understand passion. They may pretend to but you can tell the truth from their eyes."

All this time that I was dumping on Doris, people were arriving at the estate. They'd pull up to the entrance, look around a little bit and then push a button by the gate. After saying something into the intercom, they'd hop back into their car, the gate would open and they'd drive on through. I kept reading the brochure.

"Vegetarian cuisine by Moon-Kissed Foods. No salt, no sugar, no stress. Only the best of Lunar Legumes."

"What's legume?" Tina said. "I took Spanish."

"It's vegetable in French. It goes with the 'l' in 'lunar,' " I said.

"Alliteration," Tina said for my benefit. "I remember that from Gerard Manley Hopkins. What's the name of that poem?"

" 'God's Grandeur,' " Doris said. She hadn't been a nun for nothing. "I think I remember it, actually."

Hopkins's poem

God's Grandeur

The world is charged with the grandeur of God.
It will flame out, like shining from shook foil;
It gathers to a greatness, like the ooze of oil

Crushed. Why do men then now not reck his rod?
Generations have trod, have trod, have trod;
And all is seared with trade; bleared, smeared with toil
And wears man's smudge and shares man's smell; the soil
Is bare now, nor can foot feel, being shod.
And for all this, nature is never spent;
There lives the dearest freshness deep down things;
And though the last lights off the black West went
Oh, morning, at the brown brink eastward, springs—
Because the Holy Ghost over the bent
World broods with warm breast and with ah! bright wings.

"That is so beautiful," Tina said. "I'm not even Christian and I think that's beautiful."

I have to admit that Doris said it beautifully, too. It made me love her again that she knew such a good poem by heart.

"What do you mean you're not Christian?" Doris said. "So what are you?" Doris hated priests and patriarchy only in theory. In reality, the whole thing was as much a part of her as a kidney or a lung.

"Nothing right now," Tina said. "Nothing much appeals to me."

"That's too easy," Doris said. "You can't just wait passively for some spiritual spark to drop down on you from above."

"Why not?" Tina said.

"Because it won't happen," Doris said. "You have to work on it. Throughout history people have sought answers and meaning. To be alive is to be searching."

And I think she believed all that too. She just couldn't do it herself anymore. And now, like she tried to live off me, she'd tapped poor old Tina to be her spiritual surrogate.

"Oh," Tina said. I think she liked the attention but she wasn't really feeling the call. "I have been reading a little about Buddhism."

"Good," Doris said.

And just then this silver Jeep drove up to the gate, license plate MOONPWR. A bumper sticker read THE GODDESS LIVES and I thought, a message, how cool. But I didn't say anything to Tina.

Messages are to be noticed on your own, not pointed out by helpful passersby.

A short blond woman with a single braid down her back and a tall African-American woman wearing a backwards baseball cap got out of the Jeep. But they didn't speak into the intercom. Instead the tall woman leaned the short woman against the gate, firmly but not roughly, like she knew just what she wanted.

"Lesbians," Tina said.

"Interesting," Doris said.

What happened next was definitely out of our league. The white woman started to rotate her hips against the other woman, round and round, counterclockwise mostly. The African-American woman moved the other direction and pretty soon it looked as though they were going to start a fire.

"They're having sex right there against the gate," Tina said.

And I said, "All that friction. It looks like it hurts."

Everything looked like it hurt to me ever since I'd been left the last time. People kissing on TV that new way where they both open their mouths wide and then kind of bite into each other. Heterosexual lovemaking in the movies where everybody bangs against everybody else like bumper cars. Even couples holding hands in the mall looked like it hurt. Somebody was always the wrong height and had to reach too much.

Then the one in the baseball cap slid down the gate to sit at the feet of the other one. It was evidently over.

"Hiya, gals," Doris called over to them. "Great show."

"Doris," I said.

The gals waved back and then got into their Jeep. They were both smiling.

"That was gross," Tina said. "Makes me not want to be a lesbian."

"Makes me want to be one," Doris said. It was b.s. but it was cute. Doris made me mad but she also had this ability to be everybody's friend. "It was charming," she said. "Much better than on the kitchen floor."

"Maybe it was an entering ritual for luck and happiness," I said, hoping that this interpretation would have some appeal for Tina.

"Oh, I don't know," she said. "I sort of miss my mom right now. I sort of want to go home."

And then I realized that she was so young she could say things like she missed her mom and not mean them metaphorically. She was so young that those bumps and grinds would probably stay with her for a long, long time.

"I can drive you down to the airport," Doris said.

"Oh no you don't," I said. "You two would leave me here alone so easy, wouldn't you? You'd probably get on that plane with her too, wouldn't you, Doris, and just leave my car in long-term parking?"

"Not at all," Doris said.

"I don't really want to go home all that much," Tina said. "I'm just in fear."

"In fear of what?" I said.

"In fear of being the youngest one, I guess," she said. "I mean I had my first sex two days ago," Tina said. "With a woman." And then she put her hand over her mouth because Doris wasn't supposed to know.

"I told her," I said.

"Oh good," Tina said.

"El Encanto," Doris said to show her she didn't care about the sex.

"The Enchanted Place," Tina translated.

"We were all brought here for a reason," Doris went on like a New Age guru, completely out of character. "To learn something."

"And we'll all be together," I said. "So we can give each other support." And then, even though it was totally uncool to do it, I made us all take hands for a moment. "We're friends," I said.

Tina was feeling better already. "Fear would make a good topic for a poem," she said. And we squeezed tight and then let go.

We drove up to the gate but when Tina pushed the black button in the center of the intercom, there was no answer.

"Shit," Doris said. "I do not have time for this shit." She leaned across Tina and shouted, "I do not have time for this shit."

The gate swung open.

"There," Doris said. "Now step on it, girl."

But Tina drove us in slowly, like we were part of a parade and it suddenly seemed very dark.

"Nights fall abruptly out here in the desert, don't they?" I said. Tina turned on the headlights and we followed a long driveway lined forever with palm trees. I began having a very serious anxiety fantasy complete with a houseful of starving slinky vampires and their pet wolfhounds. It occurred to me that, if this were the movies, some people wouldn't get out of this place alive. Then I saw a human bat flying into the headlights of our car.

"We must have entered a gothic horror novel by mistake," Doris said evenly as the bat approached.

"This is too much," Tina said. "I'm going to puke." And she opened the car door and she did.

"I'm just a nun in habit," the bat said, out of breath, stepping around poor Tina's mistake. "People have such unpredictable reactions. I'm Sister Dorothy." She shook all our hands. "I'm in charge of opening the gate. It's been acting up so I ran out here to make sure you got in."

"Thank you," I said. "Want a ride to the house?"

"That would be nice," she said and climbed in beside me.

"Are you a workshop member?" Doris said.

"Sister Dorothy Jenkins," Dorothy said. "Paul's daughter. I live here."

"In full habit?" Doris said.

"Doris was a nun once," I said, nodding toward her. "A Franciscan. And then she left the convent."

"Everybody in my order did too," Dorothy said. "Boo hoo. Except for me. So I moved back there, habit and all. I have another one if you'd like to borrow it," she said to Doris.

"Interesting," Doris said. I could tell she thought Dorothy was completely loony.

"So you're our greeting committee?" Tina said.

"And you're that sweet Trinity from way out west. Welcome, welcome," she said, bending and bowing like someone from Japan.

And then we got to the house. It was so big and so out of place for the middle of the desert that none of us could think of a thing to say.

"Follow me," Dorothy said after Tina parked the car. Then she ran up the wide marble steps leading to the front door.

"It looks like a Renaissance villa," Doris whispered to me. She was right. We could have been in sixteenth-century Tuscany.

"Michelangelo's only design for a home," Dorothy said. "My father had it built here by real Italian workmen. Hundreds of them. And they never left. He used to brag that he upset the entire genetic balance of the region because of them."

Doris laughed and said something about Paul thinking he was God but Dorothy didn't hear her because we'd entered the main hall which was filled with about fifty women sitting, standing, talking, smoking, sharing manuscripts. It was charming. It was Florence; it was Athens during Plato except that it was all women. I was so moved that I almost wept.

"What's the big deal?" Tina said. "It's like a girls' school or college."

"No, it's not," I said. "It's multigenerational. It's a city without men."

All of a sudden everybody was silent. Just like that. And then they all turned around and stared at me. Except it wasn't at me. It was at Blaire Bennett, who was walking in the door behind me.

She walked past me so close I could smell her. "Cinnamon," I whispered, "or roses."

"What?" Doris said.

"That's Blaire Bennett," I said. She looked so good I almost wanted to taste her too. She had a short white pageboy with little bangs, tight brown skin and a compact athlete's body. She walked slow, like she knew we'd wait.

"She can't be my age," Doris said. "Damn."

When she got to the middle of the room, she began to recite a poem, with no warning at all.

Blaire's poem

Rape

Sitting in my car in the evening,
with the top down,
my head back as I watch the stars
shooting and blinking and the moon
changing color from white to yellow,
I think about how I'm getting
old and gray with lines
fanning out from my eyes and
mouth like a shattered windshield.
And then, like a collision, there's
a man on me.
The seat breaks underneath our weight.
He has a knife.
He pulls down my pants as if
I'm a piece of fruit to be peeled.
But there are no comparisons now.
This hurts like rape, like murder.
When he's done he says,
"did you like that? did you love it?"
And I say "yes," with a particular
kind of rage.
"good," he says, and disappears into
the street.

And although I would happily have
slit his throat,
Or sliced off his sex,
I say "yes" again
because already I'm
Wanting to run rapids,
Or love you again,
Before it's too late.

And then she finished and there was silence again and Blaire
seemed to be staring at me.

"She's staring at you," Tina said.

"No, she isn't," I said.

But, it was a true miracle. She walked toward me and said, "You remind me of someone." And then she walked out the same door she'd just walked in.

"It wasn't that great a poem," Doris said. "Especially at the end."

I just looked at her. How anybody could judge Blaire Bennett's poetry I'd never understand. I mean she'd won a Pulitzer, for God's sake.

Then the tallest woman in the world approached us and said, "Hello." She had curly blond hair, an English accent and the firmest handshake I'd ever felt. She was extreme and she was beautiful. "I'm Juliet Wright, the director," she said.

"We're . . . ," we said.

"I know," she said. "You're our last arrivals. Here's your information packet. Dinner in half an hour. Your names are on your doors upstairs." And then she kissed each one of us on the top of our heads.

"What was that?" Tina said as we staggered with our bags up the curving staircase to the bedroom wing.

"It's an old British custom," Doris said.

"It is?" Tina said.

"Of tall people," I said.

"Oh," Tina said. "Oh, I get it. You're teasing me again. Listen, I can't help it that I'm young. You're both being really ageist, you know. And I'm getting tired of it." Then she left us behind to go look for her room.

Doris's door label said "Doris Hamilton—smoker—eassayist." After I put her bags inside she closed the door in my face. I didn't care. Forget intense friendships. Forget cigarettes even. I was me—nonsmoker—poet. I was about to embark on a silent retreat of the soul.

My label didn't say anything about my addictions or my writing interest at all. Either I wasn't good enough or they'd run out of ink before they got to my door. I decided to think the latter. I also decided to think that Doris had closed the door on me, not because she didn't like me but because she wanted a secret drink. It's pretty easy to feel happy once you get the knack of looking at things from the opposite side. You just have to remember not to look too hard once you get there.

I walked into my room and everything was just as I had expected it would be. Twin bed, desk in front of window, moonlight, sink, mirror, lamp, curtains. It was a tiny, monastic room as if Paul Jenkins was well into his priest phase by the time he got to designing the upstairs of the house.

When I turned on the light I saw something I hadn't expected. Sitting in the middle of my pristine, white, twin bed, smiling as mysteriously as the Cheshire cat was Blaire Bennett. Buck naked.

"Hi," I said. "I think this is my room." Blaire didn't move. It occurred to me that maybe she was sitting zazen or something. Her body, I couldn't help but notice, was good, damn good, for somebody sixty years old. She was tan all over and her skin still hung close to her muscles.

"You work out?" I said, just to make conversation. Her eyes were closed but I figured she couldn't have been dead and be sitting up at the same time. Besides, without any clothes on I could see her abdomen moving in and out when she breathed. Blaire Bennett sitting naked in my room. I checked my name on the door once more to be sure.

"Come sit next to me," she said, opening her eyes and looking at me for the first time.

It was too strange. I kept standing in the doorway next to my name.

"Who do you think I am?" I said, gently. This behavior wasn't just eccentric; this was certifiably crazy.

Blaire said my name as if that would clear it all up.

I stared at her and she stared at me. I thought—she's probably on the edge of some sad brain disease and she's calling out for help. But why me?

"You look like someone I once knew," Blaire said. "It's a message I think I should take seriously."

"I like messages," I said. "Did you possibly know my mother? People say there's a strong resemblance there."

It was probably a line that had worked for her lots of times before but I didn't mind. I was flattered that she was using it on

me. And she sure was handsome. I noticed that her eyes were
deep green. And her great body seemed especially made for survival, not for debilitating mental illness. When she reached out
her hand I decided, what the hell, and I went and sat down next
to her.

"Blaire, I don't get what's going on," I said. I was sitting so
close to her that I was now sure about the cinnamon.

"I am not a nice person," she said.

"I am," I said.

"I don't concern myself with the needs of others," she said.

"I do," I said. But I wasn't taking this part of the conversation
very seriously. People are notoriously inaccurate when judging
their own basic humanity.

"I like taking risks," she said. "You don't."

"How do you know that?" I said. "Coming to this conference
is a big risk."

"You brought two friends along just in case," she said. "So it
isn't a risk at all. They are your friends, aren't they? That old
woman and the small child?"

"Actually none of us is speaking right now," I said. "And we're
all exactly twenty years apart."

"I don't go in for fine distinctions," Blaire said.

"Of course you do," I said. "You're a poet." She liked that. She
liked the way I kept contradicting her. She took my hand and
held it in hers. Me, sitting here, holding hands with a naked Pulitzer Prize–winning poet. I looked down at her thigh.

"Is that a tattoo or a birthmark?" I said.

"It's a tattoo, certainly," Blaire said. "It's a treasure chest of secrets. Even if we made love here on this bed before dinner you
still wouldn't know a thing about me. Not a thing."

"Well, of course not," I said. "Making love is the most imper-
sonal thing in the world. Besides, what's to hide? Most people
don't have a clue about what's going on inside themselves in the
first place."

"Cynical, cynical," Blaire said, patting me on my own right
thigh. But, already she was looking at me differently, like maybe
I was smart enough to talk to. One thing seemed sure, for some
reason she needed me. Badly. And, although that alone should

have sent me, the celibate social isolate, screaming from the room, I stayed. I stayed, all poised and ready to fall.

"Reminds me of that Hawthorne story, 'The Minister's Black Veil,'" I said. "Secret sin, remember that? He preaches these powerful sermons about secret sin from behind this piece of thin gray gauze. Ironically, the women parishioners find the veil a real turn-on."

"They found it a turn-on," Blaire said, "because it made him a sinner, human and flawed. Evil is always sexy." And then she outlined her treasure chest with a moistened finger so that the colors brightened considerably.

I thought, this is the woman for me.

I could tell her my secrets and all it would do is turn her on. I could fill her treasure chest up to the brim.

Of course, after my initial shock, her being naked made Blaire more approachable too. That must have been why I was talking so much. Plus, it was totally clear that all her bravado was a cover for something else. Like fear?

"You've got a great face," I said. "Good bones." I was talking about her face because I was trying not to look at anything else.

"So do you," she said, "for someone who doesn't like to take risks."

"So who do I remind you of?" I said.

"This woman I knew when we were both about your age. Like me, she wasn't very nice either," she said. "We were a good pair."

"You were lovers?" I said.

"No," Blaire said. "I didn't know about women lovers then. I barely knew about love."

"Listen," I said, "back to taking risks. I've risked having several relationships in my life, now I'm risking living alone."

"Because you got left," Blaire said. "Getting left is the opposite of risking."

"Not necessarily," I said. And then I said, "I bet you've left a few."

She smiled, pleased with that.

"Besides how can you be so sure I was the one who got left?" I said. Then I decided I didn't want to know the answer. "Never mind," I said. "Let's just say it was a lucky guess."

Blaire thought I was angry. She hung on to me like she thought I was going to go off somewhere. She said, "Never mind. I'm confrontational by nature."

"I don't know why you're here," I said.

Finally, she let go of my hand and stood up. For a moment, I was staring directly into her pubic hair. It was almost easier than her eyes.

"I can't write anymore," Blaire said, looking at me hard.

I was quiet out of artistic respect. Then I said, "Nothing?"

"Nothing that isn't crap," she said.

"Your rape poem . . ." I said.

"Is crap. Pure crap. Puerile crap," she said.

I guess I'm just a sucker for people with writer's block because at that moment I stood up and kissed her on her bony cheek.

"No pity," she said, but I think it made her feel better because she started putting her clothes on, white shorts, boots, T-shirt.

"Your rape poem had some good lines," I said. "About the wrinkles cracking like a windshield." I was more than willing to love Blaire Bennett if it would help the future of literature. I was willing to love her even if it wouldn't.

"I want you," she said from the doorway and I thought how stupid it was to get all involved with somebody who was so busy exploiting me, even before she knew who I was. And how typical. Then I thought, why not? Everything has to start someplace. And with me and Blaire, the only direction a relationship could go was up.

10

What was it exactly that made me think the stuff Blaire did was marvelous when I wouldn't put up with it from anybody else for a minute? Rubbing my hand, for God's sake. Sitting on my bed naked and complaining about her fading talents. Showboating in the entrance hall. Not that she was older and not that she was great looking. Not even that she had writer's block and I was an inveterate rescuer. What was it that made me want to turn myself inside out for a woman like Blaire just to keep her in the same room?

She was famous.

That was a new one.

"I like your writing," she said to me at dinner. "I've moved you into the afternoon seminar. The directors made a mistake putting you in the morning, certainly."

She'd won a Pulitzer.

She'd been on the cover of magazines.

People paid money to hear her speak.

And to read her poems.

If I was her girlfriend I could walk into classy gatherings on her arm and I would be important too. Who cared that I was only around to be her Calliope, the muse of poetry, the person who would love her over her writer's block? Don't forget that relationships without real intimacy fit me like a glove. I'd love her the way I wanted to be loved. All I had to do to make it work was spin in circles until I got so dizzy I couldn't tell which of us was which.

"My writing," I said glassily. "I actually came to the workshop to fall in love. I'm a complete fraud."

She didn't say anything else. She began to eat her vegetarian lasagna as if it were terrific drugs or somebody's body. At least that's what it looked like to me.

11

"Love is just another word for projection," the expert said. "The kind of love in stories, anyway."

"The good thing about poetry is that you can compare love with something else and it's short," said Jean.

"Lesbian love hasn't been overwritten," said Sonnie. She was getting all heated up. "Lesbian writers are inventing a whole new literature."

"Only if it's done well," said the expert. I hated her. I hated experts, especially if they weren't famous. And this one wasn't. She was one of us.

"The great lesbian love story has yet to be written," I said, just for the hell of it.

"You gonna write it?" the expert said.

"No," I said, passing the lasagna. "I'm going to live it."

Somebody smirked but I didn't care. The people I was talking to were so dumb they didn't even notice that I was making fun of them. Nobody looked any good to me except Blaire, who'd, thankfully, already left the table.

There were a few straight women at the workshop but mostly the fifty or so of us were lesbians. I had a feeling that being with all these lesbians together in one place was going to be damn difficult for Doris. Hardly anybody was hiding a thing which you don't see much out in the real world.

You don't see women with big, big breasts wearing sleeveless muscle shirts without bras; you don't see women with lots of flowing armpit hair and leg hair wearing shorts and raising their arms to greet the sun; you don't see groups of women talking loud and laughing and looking everybody right in the eye. I know for a fact that Doris shaves her legs every day. And she once told me that armpit hair on women is antisocial.

"For the next week I want you to consider sublimation," Vera was now saying to all of us as a group. Vera was Juliet's assistant and her lover and she'd just stepped up to the podium at the front of the room for announcements.

"You're all away from home, in this beautiful setting with these beautiful women. I call on you to avoid the temptation," she said.

"Hang it up, Vera," called out Bobbie Jones—fiction, evidently an old-timer, from two tables behind me.

Juliet got up and stood beside Vera protectively. She was about a foot taller and I tried to imagine them doing it. Juliet on top, the two of them side by side, Vera's face between Juliet's long, long legs.

"What Vera means," Juliet said, "is to think about keeping your energy for yourself. And for your writing. Don't give everything away."

Almost everybody in the room hollered with laughter.

It sounded like a fine idea to me. In theory.

12

Obsessional love is everywhere these days. Films about steely blondes stalking family men and their comfortable dogs; computer guys staking out the beloved's home, work, favorite hiking trail; a loser woman fan getting into the living room of the female cop star even, only to be sent straight to jail.

It used to be thought of as love writ larger than life, the noble love of poets and abdicating kings. The perfect love of dreamers and Olympian gods and little girls for their fathers. Now we know the truth. Obsessional love is as sick as it gets.

But how good it feels. At least at first. It gives you something to think about while you're falling asleep or while you're making love with somebody you don't like much. It helps pass the time during boring lectures and makes a ringing telephone a real event. And if the obsessional love object actually looks your way or calls you up, well, you have to admit, that's a better high than heroin.

At first I didn't exactly know that I was obsessed with Blaire. When I fell asleep that night dizzy from replaying the naked bedroom scene several dozen times, adding and subtracting crucial phrases and glances, I thought I was just excited about meeting a famous poet. When I dreamed about Blaire laughing at me with Juliet and Vera and then calling me over to them with an imperious wag of her index finger, I thought I was just nervous about my performance in the poetry workshop.

All night I sweated and twisted my sheet into a thick rope. I forgot where I was. I actually considered finding Blaire's room and knocking on her door. I wondered if a sound I heard was Blaire knocking on mine.

I woke up exhausted at 6 A.M., a full hour and a half before breakfast, in my clammy single bed. There was a deep silence. The perfect time for writing a poem, but evidently, not for me. I was staring at the ceiling, busy making the lines and discolorations into the tattoo on Blaire's leg.

Why hadn't she come to me? Why hadn't she called me to her? Had she found somebody else already, somebody she met at that evening meeting? Had she forgotten who I was, already?

The slimy downside of the land of obsessional love. And I'd only met Blaire the day before.

I knew the geography by heart. It was a land I had visited often. Those girlfriends of mine were always the perfect tour guides. See, you can't have much of an obsession if the object is both available and real at the same time. And all I ever seemed to want were unavailable con artists. I must have enjoyed the challenge of getting them to notice me, even if I never won.

Which is why, when I saw Blaire pacing on the sandy ground underneath my window I got back in bed and pulled the covers tight over my head.

My poem #4

On Not Being Able to Breathe

Taking a full breath
is an art, an act of courage.
Just ask any amphibian
or the guy in the hospital smock
his butt shriveled in the breeze
waiting for news from the lab.
Or a mountain climber near the
top of Annapurna

with the entire team
counting on her
back at base camp
because her attempt is their attempt,
supposedly.
Or when you're a child
in the surf
and a wave knocks you off your father's
shoulders.
You roll around and around
under water watching up through
the green glass for his
hands to dip you out
and when he finally does
you know you will never forgive him.

13

An hour later I got up and looked out my window again. Blaire Bennett was gone and I was beginning to contemplate not leaving my room the entire time I was here. I could spend my days looking out my window like this and sublimating. But then I realized I had nothing to sublimate into. I wasn't a real writer or artist or anything. And I had a definite feeling that the only way I was ever going to love right was to keep on practicing.

Tina came in to walk me to breakfast. I was sitting on my crummy, sweaty bed. I told her to look out my window and tell me what she saw.

"Two naked women kissing," she said, turning back to me. She didn't even act very interested, which seemed both good and bad. Then I realized she was making it up.

"Oh, come on," I said. I was sitting on my bed putting on a pair of socks.

"Okay," she said. "Doris walking back and forth in a nun's habit."

"That's a good one too," I said and I went over to look out. There indeed was Doris in a nun's habit, pacing like Blaire had been. It couldn't have been anyone else. "But there weren't any naked women, were there, Tina?"

"Yes," Tina said. "Doris must have scared them off. That garden's not technically a clothes-optional area, is it?"

"What the hell is Doris doing?" I said.

"She must have taken Sister Dorothy up on her offer," Tina said.

"Why?" I said.

"Why not?" Tina said. "She's reworking her unresolved convent experience. She's giving it her best shot."

"For God's sake," I said. Tina's precocity was beginning to get on my nerves.

"You should be proud of her," Tina said.

"It's so bizarre," I said. "It's so public." I looked down at Doris. She was fingering something, possibly rosary beads.

"The personal is public," Tina said.

"Oh, leave it alone," I said. "That's not the right phrase anyway."

"I fine-tuned it," Tina said. "Give me a break. Writers are supposed to uninhibitedly let their instincts run free. You can always edit later."

"Ah, Tina," I said. "I taught you well." She laughed. I knew I wouldn't be able to get away with that much longer especially after Blaire got ahold of her. Blaire would probably make my teaching look like white bread or vanilla yogurt. And with that thought I had a moment of healthy rivalry while I forgot to be obsessed.

"My back hurts," I said, sitting down on the bed. "This mattress is not that great for sleeping. And Doris is embarrassing. Don't you think her behavior kind of reflects on us?"

"Let's go eat," Tina said, with no sympathy at all. She looked out the window. Her stomach growled.

"You're not still growing or anything, are you?" I said. It was a hideous thought, that someone who was my friend could be that young.

At breakfast, I was happy, I truly was. I put Blaire and Doris on the back burner and just listened. Nobody was talking about writing anymore. It was all—who did it last night, or this morning, possible time sequences, sexual dynamics, positions and now-what's. We were suddenly in life instead of babbling on about how we were going to corner it and make it do what we wanted on paper.

Of course there were a few who raced up to their rooms and started word-processing their experience right away.

Jean's chapter one

Fake Love

After the poetry reading, Sarah went outside to look at the stars. They were particularly bright in the desert and she wanted to memorize the position of all the constellations to tell her lover, June, who had stayed back home in the city.

Suddenly she gasped. She saw her first shooting star streak through the sky.

"It's so beautiful," she whispered.

"So are you," said a voice, coming up behind her.

Sarah giggled. She knew who it was. It was Jennifer, a published poet, who had sat next to her at the reading and made snide comments about the rather obvious nature imagery of the woman reading before her.

"You're just a shooting star, that's what you are, you're just a shooting star . . ." Jennifer sang, loud and off-key.

"I don't even know you," Sarah said. "You're embarrassing me." But she liked it. She liked it because June would never, ever know anything about what she did during the five days and nights of this women's writers' conference.

"Let's go sit down over there and tell each other our lives," Jennifer said. "And then let's go upstairs and show each other our bodies."

And Sarah knew she would do whatever Jennifer wanted because that was the nature of the thing. And she knew none of it would be real or sincere or honest because that was the nature of the thing too. And, as she took Jennifer's hand and led her to the chairs where they would make up stories about their lives, she smiled because this fake love was going to be so hot.

And Blaire was there too, at breakfast, sitting with Juliet and Vera. That was fine with me, because they weren't rival girlfriends and Blaire was smiling. At me, I thought.

"Blaire Bennett smiled at you," Tina said, eating her fruit, yogurt and granola out of a white bowl as fast as she could.

"Are you sure?" I said. "You're so busy eating."

"She likes you. I can tell," Tina said. "Remember I'm on to this student-teacher stuff."

"You didn't like me that way," I said.

"I might have," she said, "but I controlled it. For the larger good."

"Good," I said, smiling back at Blaire.

Doris sat down with us after everybody else left, for coffee. In spite of being such a joke she looked better this way than she had in a while. Maybe the habit was kind of pulling her together into a unified whole. Maybe it was because of how much it covered.

"Blaire was sitting in my room with no clothes on when I got there last night," I said. "She has writer's block."

"And she wants you to be her muse," Doris said.

"Exactly," I said.

"In the main hall she said that you reminded her of someone," Tina said. "I bet she's gripped by a compulsion to work her stuff for that person out on you. That was the plot of this made-for-TV movie a couple of months ago. It was based on a true story where this woman murdered her husband during one of her flashbacks because she thought he was her abusive father."

"She undoubtedly got put in jail for it too," Doris said.

"She did," Tina said. "She couldn't prove it had been part of a flashback."

"No," I said. "What we've got here is a person panicked by loss of creative force. What we've got here is someone who is facing something none of us can even imagine. A loss without parallel in average life. Not even the death of a child or another loved one can compare."

"Oh really," Doris said.

It was obvious that I'd overdone it but that didn't stop me.

"If you lose a spouse or a child you still have yourself, but if you're Blaire Bennett and you can't write anymore, well, you're losing your very essence," I said. And then I felt pretty shitty. I mean, who was I to lecture Doris, whose husband after all, died right in her arms?

"And now you've got to save her?" Doris said.

I couldn't answer her. As usual, she'd hit the nail right on the head. When you're determined to repeat all your same mistakes over and over again what's there left to say?

"What's with the habit?" I finally said.

"I don't know," Doris said. Then she pushed a couple of tears away with her thumb. "I never know what I'm feeling. I get a stomachache and then it's over."

"Or you have a drink," I said.

"Or I have a drink," she said, picking up her coffee.

"Wait," I said.

"Okay," she said and then there was a long, terrible silence while Doris tried to understand her feeling. Finally she said, "I think what I'm feeling is sad." Then there was another long pause. "Because there are certain things I miss about being a nun," she said, crying a little bit. "Like Mary Harold and Mary John." And that was all for now. She took a slug of coffee like it was Scotch and said, "Thank you."

We all sat companionably for a while in silence while I remembered this horrible antivivisection film I watched by mistake on the public access station. At first there was this nice woman who was holding a sick monkey and then the camera showed her tease it while it looked up at her desperately, white drool coming from its mouth. In the next scene they'd put its head in a box and were evidently giving it electric shock, because the rest of its body kept convulsing. Then the film was replaced by the antivivisection speaker who made his point about the disgusting nature of animal torture.

For days, all I could see was that monkey, head bent back, limbs flaccid, looking up at that woman who was laughing at the camera.

And the seagull, standing on one leg with something hanging out of its beak, hooked in for life.

And the dead deer, dragged down the hiking trail by hunters

carrying crossbows, wearing bloodstained camouflage pants because you have to cut out some gland right away or the meat gets ruined.

"You okay?" Doris said. "It's good probably that Blaire's strong on you."

"Good?" I said. "We don't even know each other. It's not remotely a real thing."

"She has to make something happen so she'll feel alive," Doris said.

"But what do I get out of it?" I said, thinking about all those wasted animals. "She'll use me, then she'll drop me. All I am is a victim of life."

"What do you have to lose?" Doris said. "At the very least you'll have a great story."

"And what good's a story?" I said. "When it only makes you look bad."

My Poem #5

Women Who Love Men

A heterosexual woman I know
Wants something from me.
She wants to suck on my breast.
She wants to put two fingers into
The warm sea cave between my legs.
She wants to lie against me in bed
My soft stomach supporting
The small of her back.
She doesn't want me.
Just my stomach and breasts and vagina
Like a narcotic or a vacation
Or a mother.
And I am afraid of her.

14

My poems were taking on this tone of cold steel. Something was beginning to come to me about my inner life and damned if I could do anything to stop it. I spent the rest of the morning writing in my journal and trying to get back to normal. But everything I thought about to write was worse than the thing before.

My Journal

The Tennis Pro

In my dream I was making love to a young blond tennis pro (a cuter Monica Seles) who had somehow missed out on experiencing the wonders of orgasm. When I touched her she was delighted but when I put my mouth to her the smell was so strong that I couldn't stay. She didn't seem to notice. Like most athletes she saw her body as a piece of equipment, not as an extension of her soul. When she touched me, her fingers hurt. I pulled them out and took a look. Her long fingernails were blood red. And then I woke up.

A couple of hours later, I sat down next to Blaire at lunch. Nobody said a word. She just kept shoveling the thin vegetable soup

made from last night's green beans and carrots into her mouth.
She didn't look so pretty right now. She looked kind of old and
tested, twice-cooked like the vegetables in the soup, all the vita-
mins boiled out of them long ago.

Poor, poor Blaire. The burden of her creative gift seemed suddenly insupportable. How could she do her art all these years
without going a little bit mad, without eating herself up from the
inside out? In spite of all my instincts toward self-preservation,
my ugly and incipient inner life, I'd still give her my guts if she'd
have them.

"Blaire, you have a secret you want to tell me, don't you?" She
put her hand on my thigh and pressed. I couldn't make out the
message exactly. I didn't know if she had a secret to tell or if
she wanted to keep them all locked up tight, but it was someplace for us to begin. I still hadn't the faintest idea what was
going on inside her head.

"I have a secret to tell you too," I said.

Somebody passed the chicken, a concession to the non-
vegetarians, but it was even more anemic than the soup. Everybody seemed to be listening to me, but nobody was really, maybe
not even Blaire.

"My story is that I thought I might at last have a famous lover
which is probably what I've wanted all along," I said. "But all
along all I've gotten are losers with famous personalities, narcis-
sists with nothing to show for all their talk. I end up spending
the money and providing the patience and concern. And when
they leave me, and they do always leave me, they take my things
with them to keep out the cold and pass the time."

Blaire stirred. Maybe she was listening. Why not? There wasn't
anything else to listen to except me and the people in the
kitchen dishing up the sugar-free apple betty. She took off the
silver chain she was wearing around her wrist and handed it to
me like I'd passed some test or something.

And I hadn't even had to tell her my really big secret, the icky
bad one about driving my mother into the tree.

"Does this mean we're going steady?" I said. "Do I get to keep
it or what?" Maybe this was what was good about finding a real

famous lover at last. Maybe Blaire had something left over to give to me.

"Sure," Blaire said. "What the hell."

At that moment, everybody in the room started talking at once.

15

She did turn out to be a terrific lover which I wasn't expecting at all. It was almost enough for me that she was famous and had handed me a silver bracelet right off her wrist. But now she was the kind of lover who made you feel you were really the one she was making love to.

Which was a good thing because I kept forgetting who I was.

When you make love with a new person, maybe it's always that way. You're different because you're working from a new script or writing one as you go. So how did Blaire know that I liked my breasts touched just that way with the palms of her hands rubbing in circles and then pressing down hard so they were almost flat? How did she know that I liked talk in sex, not silence, and lots of kissing? How did she know that I didn't want her to bite my earlobe or breathe in my ear?

And when we were finished (after we'd both cried a little), and were eating the room service vegetable quiche she'd ordered from Lunar Legumes, in Paul Jenkins's big master bedroom, how did she know to ask me about my mother?

"Why do you ask?" I said. She looked at me. "I'm sorry," I said. "But it's not my favorite subject. Do you think that just because you're older, I have a mother fixation?"

"Nothing so obvious," Blaire said. "Your eyes are sad. When you make love. Particularly when you look at me." She took a sip of champagne. Someone had brought her a bottle and now she was sharing it with me. I finished my quiche and then some of hers. I was hungrier than usual and floating a little bit too. I had no idea what to say next.

"Oh," I said.

"Maybe you would like to hit me or hurt me," she said. "Maybe you would like to humiliate me in some sexual way."

"What?" I said. "Do you like that?" I couldn't imagine it from the way she had just been with me. But maybe S and M was the way she made space. That's exactly the way sex always is. After you have it you know your lover even less than you did before.

"Not particularly," Blaire said. "Maybe you want me to do that to you."

"I love you," I said.

"What?" she said.

"I said I love you," I said. "I'm easy. I'm easily moved."

"I'm too old for love," she said.

"Oh," I said. If she wanted to pretend to tell me the truth, I'd pretend to believe her. I knew that game by heart. It's the shaky foundation all relationships sit on, even though everybody swears it's bedrock for sure.

"If I could love somebody it would probably be you," Blaire said. I smiled at her. It was a lot better than nothing.

"Why?" I said.

"Because you give everything you've got," she said.

I kissed her then and stroked her cheek.

I wanted more but I knew I couldn't push it. I just hoped to hell whatever she had would be worth the wait.

16

I left Blaire's room that night around ten and spent the next few hours smelling her on my fingers and thinking about lovemaking until I couldn't stand it anymore. The next morning I finally took a deep breath and looked out my window at the desert landscape.

I could see a lot because the colors were still strong and the sun wasn't high enough yet to bleed them dry. I realized that I'd been so busy losing myself into Blaire the past couple of days that I hadn't even watched these changes or noticed what the desert animals were doing or appreciated how everything adapted to the heat. And then I started feeling a little sad. Here I was missing out on all these important things just because I had to keep looking for somebody to love.

17

"Dale's been thinking about short hair," Tina said, later that morning, "like mine." We were sitting out on the veranda with a bunch of other women who were writing or talking or reading in the clear bright sun. Tina had been switched to the afternoon workshop like me so we had time to kill.

"Good idea," I said. "You're going to save the braid though, aren't you?"

"I was Blaire's girl last year," Dale said, fingering the tip. "Tina wanted me to tell you. I wouldn't have otherwise." Dale was the short white half of the couple we'd watched humping against the front gate a few days ago. She was cute, like Tina and about ten years older.

Tina had some salon-quality scissors in her hand which she was opening and closing, ready to go. "Sit down," she said to Dale, pointing at a little stool.

"You brought your own scissors?" I said.

"I always do," she said, "like a toothbrush. I learned to cut hair at Girl Scout camp when I was fourteen. One of the counselors was Jon Peters's daughter. I'll do you next, if you want. I'll do anybody."

"I want to pay you," Dale said. "This is a big job. Big responsibility."

"So what are you telling me?" I said.

"That Blaire picked me up at writing camp last year. And we were lovers for a while. Different place altogether. A wooded retreat in Maine. Intellectual crowd. Smith and Radcliffe alums, that whole thing."

Tina undid the braid, combed out the hair and then began to snip, layer by layer, very slowly. Blond wisps began to gather around Dale's feet. I felt kind of sick.

"So why are you here?" I said.

"She's a good teacher," Dale said.

"That's enough reason for me," Tina said, not taking her eyes off her work. Dale was becoming positively pre-Raphaelite, waves of hair softly floating around her cheeks and neck.

"Blaire wasn't that real to me," she said. "She was easy to get over."

All of a sudden I slugged her in the bicep like a buddy.

"Watch it," Tina said. "I'm doing the crown."

Dale was full of shit but I liked her anyway. For one thing, we were practically related from both having slept with Blaire, and for another, she did remind me of me. I understood her. She was kind of a bitch but with the big heart of a natural victim.

"Maybe it never happened at all," Dale said. And then she went to the bathroom to look at herself in the mirror.

I followed her.

"You traveled all this way just to see Blaire Bennett again?" I said. I stood next to her and looked into the mirror at her, into her eyes. It was very confusing. It was like looking at a person from their own point of view, from inside their skin.

"We're okay now," she said. "We're friends."

"Swell," I said. It wasn't exactly like I thought Blaire and I would be married or anything and I didn't totally mind being used to crack her writer's block but I didn't much like being part of a pattern.

"Do me next," I said to Tina when I walked back out to the veranda.

"No," Tina said.

"Why not?" I said. "You did her, you can do me."

"No," she said. "You're doing it to be mad. You're thinking—if Blaire was with Dale, how special can I be?"

I told her to be quiet because Dale was coming back out.

"I want to pay you," Dale said. "I look so different."

"No," Tina said.

"All kids need money," she said.

"I said no," Tina said.

I sat down on the stool and just waited for something to happen. When Dale left, Tina sat down at my feet like maybe I'd changed and I still had something decent to teach her.

"Well," I said.

Tina looked up expectantly. She'd been pissed off at me for a couple of days because of how far and how fast I'd fallen for Blaire and now she was giving me another chance.

The trouble was I didn't want another chance at all. I still wanted to follow this thing to the end, wherever that was and figure it out from there. And I wanted Tina and Doris to stick around while I did it, like guardian angels or saints. But I didn't tell Tina any of that for obvious reasons, the main one being that it was just plain sick.

18

Which is when I decided it was time to go home. Cut my losses.
Blow some wind around my brain. Get celibate again. Join a goddess group. Any group. A therapy group. Forget Blaire and her
creative insecurities. Return the silver bracelet. Forget Dale and
how she couldn't let go.

But I was too lazy to repack. Stupid me.

The afternoon poetry workshop was hell because I was such a
lousy poet. The other participants were fairly generous but it was
only too clear that I was out of my league. Tina wasn't great either but she was catching on so fast she was whipping off complete stanzas after each criticism and then saying, "You mean
like this?" when her turn came up next.

Today was worse than the day before when all we had to do
was introduce ourselves and read poems of famous poets that
Blaire had brought to class. She'd known everybody: Rich and
Plath and Sexton and Snodgrass and Lowell and some of the
younger ones as well. She talked about the importance of dis-
cussing both technique and the emotions and psychology behind
the work. She told us the ground rules: Never interrupt, always
ask the writer first what she wants in response and don't show off
while pretending to be helpful.

Today we had to read our poems and I realized that after

Blaire really looked at my work, it was impossible that she would have any feeling for me whatsoever.

My poem #6

>   Maybe if I didn't live alone with three cats
>   I wouldn't need to watch them
>   Sleep, whiskers twitching in their dreams.
>   Or wonder what they are thinking
>   When we look into each other's eyes,
>   For minutes sometimes.
>   Do they think about me?
>   When I touch myself they like to sit
>   On my chest and purr
>   Sweetly, for they are both sex and women.
>   I know who they are
>   These cats, these gifts.
>   They are familiars
>   And they can see in the dark.

We were supposed to write a poem during our free time that morning about something or someone that we loved. Tina wrote about me, her favorite English teacher, which was probably her way of giving me another pep talk so I would start being her role model again or at least somebody she could respect. I nodded warmly at her when she read it, pretending to be the old me, the one with self-esteem and objectivity.

Dale wrote about the woman she was with now, a long metaphorical piece about darkness and passion that seemed vaguely racist. I didn't say anything because Dale hadn't wanted a response from anybody, and respecting that was one of Blaire's ground rules.

Blaire wasn't even bothering to avoid my eyes or treat me with exaggerated indifference to cover our real relationship. That, of course, made me wonder if we had one at all. If anything, she was paying more attention to me than she was the others, probably because she was pitying me and trying to let me down easy.

"Life is about having secrets and deciding which ones to tell and which ones to keep," Blaire said. "In poetry you have to make decisions too. But the most important thing is that you have to tell your secrets. Anything less isn't worth writing about." I knew what was coming next. We were going to have to tell each other secrets for practice. I wasn't a teacher for nothing.

Relationships were like poetry, which is why I'd never told anybody about that car accident. I'd never had a relationship worth the energy. But I made a big decision. I'd tell about it today, in Blaire's class, to Blaire and then I'd see what happened. Maybe it would be good.

I'd tried to kill my mother by driving recklessly down a dark country road at night with her in the passenger seat. I was very conscious of what I was doing when I did it as well as the chance I was taking with my own life. I ran us into a tree and totaled the car, my car, and she broke her nose on the dashboard and bled all over her new blue silk shirt. I never spoke to her again after the hospital and she didn't try to contact me either.

What if the class asked me why I had tried to kill my mother? The secret that I'd tried to do it should have been enough. But, if I had to actually explain it, I could say that she didn't treat me like I wanted her to and that, having given up on changing her, I figured I would be better off without any mother at all. It was much more complicated but what did they want? This wasn't therapy.

Blaire outsmarted me. We weren't supposed to tell each other our secrets right now. We were supposed to make up a false secret to mix up with a real secret and then she'd tell us what to do next. Sometimes I made assignments like that too, to sort of blunt the intensity of the truth by making it part of a game.

I wrote down two secrets on a piece of paper and then tore it in half. The first one said "I tried to kill my mother" and the other one said "I want to kill Blaire." I peeked at Tina's. One said "I am a lesbian" and the other one said "I am a lesbian." Everybody was either writing or thinking or tearing paper in half. Nobody looked scared at all.

Blaire said, "Now you are to think about what the false secret and the real secret have in common."

"Then what?" I said.

"Then you know something about yourself you didn't know before," she said. "The connection between the two things you just wrote down. Pass them all to me and I'll read them out loud," Blaire said, "anonymously."

Tina said, "I want to do it. I think it sounds interesting. I trust everybody here."

"You would," I said. Kids were so easy, easier than me, even.

"We'll mix all the secrets up so nobody will know who actually wrote each one. Is that okay with everybody?" Blaire asked.

She collected our secrets and our lies and then read them aloud to us in pairs. She told us that nobody should do anything no matter what, but when she got to mine I felt so much I almost couldn't sit still. I was sad not for what I'd done. I'd accepted my basic feral nature a long time ago. What I was sad about was that hearing my secret from the outside made me realize not how much I hated her but how much I still wanted a mother I could love.

19

After the class Tina and I went for a drive to buy some more Scotch for Doris. Thinking about Blaire had become unpleasant, like that feeling of someone sexually touching you too long and too insistently in one place. Besides, nothing at all had happened after I'd told such an enormous secret. Blaire hadn't even looked at me when the class was done.

"Do you want to go home still?" I asked Tina. I loved being with Tina right now, away from El Encanto. It was real life again. I watched the brown and red landscape and the strange cactus out the car window while I waited for her to answer me.

"No," she said. "I'm learning a lot. I just wish there were more people my own age to hang out with."

That hurt my feelings but I figured I deserved it after going so crazy about Blaire.

"Did you honestly try to kill your mother?" she said then in spite of Blaire's admonition that we weren't supposed to talk about the secrets outside of class.

"How did you know that was me?" I said.

"Because of the way you looked when she read it," Tina said. "Your mouth got tight. And besides, who else would have written the false secret that went with it about killing Blaire Bennett?"

I wondered how to answer her. To tell more of the truth or to tell more of a lie? I wondered which would be better for Tina and better for me. And because they were not necessarily the same thing, I was quiet all the rest of the way to the fancy liquor store on the outskirts of town.

When we got there, I parked the car and we looked at the store which was so bright with huge windows and lights that I couldn't imagine being able to go in.

"It looks like a huge ice cube with tons of subliminal messages frozen inside," Tina said, as if we were still at the workshop and anybody cared about her lines.

I decided to answer Tina as much as I could because she had needed to ask me and I should respect that. At least that's what I told myself. Probably I was happy to finally tell somebody all about it.

"Yes," I said.

"Why?" Tina asked, looking at the bright windows and not at me.

"I hated her, Tina," I said. "She made me feel terrible all the time and I couldn't think of any other way to get rid of her from my life. Then."

"But to try to take her life," Tina said after a moment. "That's . . ." And then she stopped. I knew what she wanted to say. Something about it being not human to actually try to kill somebody. That my action put me so far out of the realm of regular human beings that she didn't know who I was anymore.

"We're all capable of these things," I said. I didn't actually know if this was true or not but was I so different from anybody else? "And you'd have to meet my mother," I said. "She's inspirational." I chuckled a little to show her I wasn't a murderer anymore.

"It isn't funny at all," Tina said sternly. "This is very difficult for me. I'm still a teenager."

"Haven't you ever wanted to hurt somebody?" I said. Didn't all teenagers want to kill someone? It was mean to turn it around on her, but I really needed some empathy to leaven the situation. Without empathy, where was there to go?

"No," Tina said, flat, without feeling. In fact, she was now looking at me through mean, slitted eyes.

"I've never even told anybody about it," I said. That didn't matter either. I gave up. "Let's just go inside," I said. "Maybe you'll feel better there."

"Inside a liquor store?" she said.

As soon as we walked in, Tina pointed toward the California Chardonnays and said, "Look at that."

It was Blaire and Dale, head to head, examining a label as if their lives depended on it. At first I wanted to just watch them but I figured I couldn't do that with Tina on my tail.

She took care of everything. "Come on," she said. "Let's go over and talk to them." So we left the copper calm of the Scotch and bourbon aisle and headed over to wine. I wasn't very happy even though the liquor store was obviously designed by some psychologist hired to get you to feel hearty and openhanded.

Life-sized cutouts of attractive and popular people toasting life were hanging from ceiling lights and standing in the aisles, deliberately obstructing customer flow. I pushed over a tanned man, leaping dog and Frisbee on our way to Blaire.

"Stop it," Tina hissed. "They're only a marketing device."

"I know that," I said. "But they're blocking my route."

"You can't always have your own way," Tina said.

"Hi," Dale said when she saw us.

"So, are you two back involved again?" I said. Tina pinched my arm.

"I can't get used to my hair," Dale said. "I keep reaching around to play with the braid."

"Like an amputation," Blaire said. I smiled. Maybe she was so nervous and guilty she could only say dumb things like that.

"I told you we were friends," Dale said.

"You don't owe me an explanation," I said to Blaire, so cool.

"I know," Blaire said, hard.

Tina was standing beside me, watching me closely. What Blaire had just said felt so bad I was suddenly almost on my knees. She'd punched all the air out of me. Here I'd given her my entire self and my biggest secret and this is what I got in return. A comment like that.

My jaw tightened and saliva poured into my mouth. I couldn't seem to swallow. I didn't know what to do. Should I let it dribble out like I'd had a sudden stroke? I spat on the ground by the sweet dessert wines on the bottom shelf.

Nobody said anything.

Now I did want to kill Blaire. Which made both secrets true. Instead I swatted a bottle of wine on the top shelf which toppled about ten other bottles onto the floor.

Everybody hopped out of the way and said, "Oh my God. What did you do that for?" I just laughed at them. They could figure it out for themselves.

Back on the highway, Tina said something different. She said, "I'm sort of beginning to understand this violence thing you have. I mean I'm beginning to appreciate it. What you did back there was pretty good. They weren't being that nice."

"You think so?" I said.

"Yes," she said. "They even made me mad."

"Thanks," I said. It was terrific to have somebody on my side.

"Are we going on a crime spree now or what?" Tina said.

"Not exactly," I said. "But I think we'll go get Doris and check out of El Encanto if it's okay with you."

"We forgot the Scotch," Tina said.

"We'll stop someplace else," I said.

"What if she doesn't want to leave?" Tina said.

"We'll make her," I said. "She's been in that habit long enough."

20

"But what did we learn?" Tina said later that night after we'd picked up our stuff and Doris. "Weren't we all supposed to learn something?"

Nobody had seemed to care much when we told them we were leaving early except for Sister Dorothy who probably had secret hopes about Doris retaking vows and joining her own teeny order. Juliet and Vera were preoccupied. A couple of the nonfiction students and one of the poets had started remembering childhood abuse experiences in response to some imprudent writing assignments and now they were wandering the grounds like suicidal zombies.

"Keep writing," Juliet had said to us as a sort of benediction, her eyes scanning the scenery over and beside our heads, just in case.

"Come back next year," Vera said, counting out low doses of somebody's Valium to buffer the writer's flashbacks until help arrived.

"I learned I can have a major uninhibited moment in a well-lit southwestern liquor store," I said now, in the car. "And that it could make me feel better than I have in months, years even."

It was true. Ever since the incident with my mother I'd kept myself on a pretty tight leash, in case I had any other latent tendencies in that direction. I didn't say it now but I also learned that telling the murder attempt out loud was very satisfying, like popping a fat and evil pimple at last.

Tina turned up the car radio and we all listened hard as if the music was going to have a special message just for us. It was a kind of jazz I'd never heard before, fast and hard but with mystery at its center. I decided that I didn't care that I was never going to get to see Blaire again. What she had to offer me didn't seem like much now, except for another big, old broken heart.

"I learned two things," Tina said. "Number one is that being relentlessly with all adults is sort of a drag. No offense. And number two, I'm still not sure about the lesbian thing."

"You're not sure?" I said. Tina was only a kid and she'd only been a lesbian that one time, but somehow I'd expected more conviction from her. Still, I can't say that I was much of a role model.

"Men may be not as good as women," she said, thinking it out, "but, because of that, they don't get your expectations up. Heterosexuality may not hurt as much as being a lesbian. You see what I mean?"

She had a good point, of course, but mostly it betrayed her youth. When is love ever subject to reason?

"I learned that there are worse things than wearing a nun's habit," Doris said.

"Like what?" I said.

"Like not wearing one," she said.

21

Of course, predictably, the next morning driving through the middle of the dry hot desert, I started really thinking about my mother for the first time in ten years. What else was there to do?

When I was a child I saw her the way all little girls see their mothers. I thought she was a goddess, a diva, a star. But I never thought of her as a saint. Even when I was in preschool I knew that she wasn't that type at all.

My mother was the sexy, wide-laughter kind of woman. The kind who smoked Viceroys, drank martinis and listened to Ella Fitzgerald sing scat. She drove a white Thunderbird convertible with a red stripe painted down the side. She wasn't a saint, like some of the other mothers were. She was much more dangerous than that. She was alive.

Of course, my mother could get killed too. By me. Being a star or being a saint for that matter, was no guarantee that your children wouldn't someday want to make you die.

It was the extremes that did it. As she hit yet another service ace, or had the walls of our dining room redecorated to look like Gertrude Stein's Paris salon complete with tiny reproduced Matisses and Picassos hung high, or told a dirty joke that sent the whole room into bottomless gales of laughter, as she spiraled off into the endless dome of sky with her style, her charm, her beauty revolving around her like stars or planets, I realized I didn't exist at all.

Mommy bashing is a drag but try to see it this way: tremendous love and hate together, all balled up and strangling, that's what I had to live with until I decided to drive us into the tree. Even though I was almost thirty at the time and we all know it's damned unattractive if you haven't stopped blaming your parents way before that, killing her still seemed like the only thing left to do. I might have changed my phone number or moved far away but to really pull her out of me, like an alien or cancer, she had to cease to exist and not just in my head.

After we hit the tree there was lots of flowing blood and several broken bones. My body ached for months even after everything was mended. My mother's forehead was cut deeply, her nose was broken and she had to have a pin in her hip. My pain made the attempted emotional surgery seem real. And I liked thinking about how miserable I'd made her.

But, ultimately, I'd failed. There wasn't any death at all.

Still, in the hospital, when I pretended that I'd lost control or fallen asleep, my mother knew. And maybe that was the silver lining. She knew. She didn't press charges or anything, but, for once, over the bandages across the bridge of her nose, she did look at me. I couldn't help but think it was too bad the big moment had to be like this.

Now, after sharing a Macho Burrito and Pepsi Special near Needles, Tina decided that the three of us were so bonded that when we got home she had to move in with me, mother-killer and liquor store vandal.

"You have great taste," I said.

"Thank you," she said.

"Doris," I said to the backseat where Doris was stretched out, barefoot, tanning her toes.

"What?" Doris said.

"Why don't you live with Doris?" I said to Tina.

"You should go to college," Doris said.

"Of course you say that," Tina said. "You're the principal."

"I'd say it anyway," Doris said.

"Then you're saying it because you don't want me living with you," Tina said. "The point is not college. It's that I want to get away from home but I don't want to go to school for a while."

"Oh," I said. "I thought you told me you were tired of older people."

Tina said, "You need me."

"No, I don't," I said, but I knew I did. Deep and intense friendships were beginning to look damned appealing once again. Plus, who's to say being Tina's other mother wouldn't have a big psychic payoff for me in the cosmic long run?

"Yes you do," Doris said. "We both do."

"But she doesn't need us," I said, which was, of course, much more to the point.

That night, in my own bed, in my own room, in my own house, I closed my eyes and saw all of the women I had loved because I'd hoped they were going to be my good mother. I didn't actually think of it that way when I'd first used them in my fantasies. At the time, it had felt like enough just to make up gentle and loving things we could do together.

Some of these mother/women I'd only seen on the street; some of them I'd worked with; one was a full-fledged movie star whose roles I knew by heart. In my fantasies, after I'd won them to me, they each loved me completely. And I loved them. They were my lovers but, of course, they were my mothers too. They listened while I talked and they kept out the cold with blankets of breasts and flesh and kisses. They always helped me fall asleep.

But they couldn't stop bad dreams. Tonight it was about the beach, where I slapped an evil little girl for keeping the huge and pathetic fish she'd caught, in her arms, so she could watch it die.

22

The next day when I went outside there were two things on my doorstep. The newspaper and Tina, looking positively waifish and dejected.

"Guess what?" Tina said. "You'll never guess."

"Your parents threw you out for being a lesbian," I said. Tina fell straight back into the ivy by my front door. I thought I was supposed to laugh.

"Ha, ha, ha," I said. I was thinking how young Tina was compared to the average person. I glanced down at the front page headline just to the left of Tina's head. It said:

"Senate votes for reduction in defense budget." "Presidency in shambles. First Lady handles press conference alone."

Tina opened her eyes. "You're right," she said. "My mother is a closet homophobe. I walked in the front door and she said, 'This is your last night under this roof.' I hate her. I wish she were dead."

I almost asked, "How did she find out?" but then I realized it didn't matter.

"No you don't," I said, instead. "Don't even think that. She did one bad thing."

"I want to kill her," Tina said.

"Are you making this up so I'll let you live here? Because I told you that about my mother?" I said.

"She's not fair," Tina said. "I've only been with one woman once."

"So what do you want, Tina?" I said.

"I just need a safe place to grow up," she said.

"Me too," I said. I knew now that it was inevitable, that Tina was going to live with me for a while whether I liked it or not. And because I was sick of being alone, I was pretty sure I'd like it a lot.

"Are you hungry?" I said.

"Yes," she said. "I'm starving."

While Tina made us scrambled eggs, sausage (our first meat in a week) and coffee, I was inspired to write.

My poem #7

On Taking a Nap

I can never sleep at night.
At night I see things
I don't want to see
Projected on a wide screen
Inside the back of my skull

But during the day
I can hold myself
In the white light that
Flows into my room
Like mother's milk
Or Kaopectate

I can think about being
Rocked in a big chair
On my mother's lap,
Which never did happen.

I can think about
Rocking my own daughter
On my lap,
Which never will.

Tina moved in and she thrived.

I thrived too. And I must admit I enjoyed having another mother-hater under the same roof, except that Tina's hate was rather situational and adolescent compared to mine. In fact I didn't think she really hated her mother at all.

"Have you talked to your mother?" I said to her one evening about a month later over a plate of stir-fry vegetables and rice. She looked tired but content because she'd been doing interesting physical labor all day at Amazon Autoworks. She was an apprentice mechanic for minimum wage, decent benefits and a bright future. It was all right with me until college but I still looked at it like learning to type with a feminist twist. Tina said I was as reactionary as her mother.

"Well have you?" I repeated. Tina was stirring her stir-fry in tight concentric circles with far too much intensity.

"No," she said. "She should call me. She's the one at fault."

"That's how it works?" I said.

"Yeah," Tina said, close to crying. "Mothers are supposed to do everything they can to retrieve their children. They must overcome pride and self-pity. It should be an organic drive."

"I guess it isn't," I said. "Or else my mother got wired backwards."

"What?" Tina said. Needless to say, she wasn't all that interested in my historical experience. She was too busy living in the present.

"My mother thinks I should come groveling to her," I said. Actually I don't think my mother cared if she ever saw me again, groveling or not, but I was trying to illustrate a point.

"Oh," she said. We sat there without talking for a while, Tina stirring and me chewing. I felt always in between parent and peer with her which wasn't half bad. I just had to keep reminding myself to give her a lot of room to move around in, and that handing her the right answer wasn't such an important thing.

"She's had over a month," Tina said.

"Reaching out to her might feel pretty good," I said. "You'd be emotionally superior."

"I don't think so," Tina said.

I had such mixed feelings they probably showed. I wanted Tina to stay and if she made up with her mother she probably wouldn't. But, I also wanted her to be happy and I knew that, estranged, she'd never be happy again.

The next day Tina moved back home. She left behind an orange kitten named Piston that she'd found hiding behind a reconditioned Toyota engine at Amazon. She didn't take anything and she hadn't lived in the guest room long but I felt as bad as I had when any lover walked out, leaving me to fend for myself.

What I missed were the comfortable things that didn't have anything to do with sleeping in the same bed. Like cooking and eating together, like telling dreams before work if you wanted to, watching television and commenting on how everything is white men, like helping with—"does this go with this?" The more intimate things that I'd had with lovers seemed strange and burdensome after Tina and far less real.

"It was a more authentic relationship than any other you've had," Doris said, over a cup of coffee in her office. It was mid-fall by this time, and the first quarter of the new school year.

"Thanks a lot," I said. "What about mine with you?"

"Excepting me, of course," she said.

"I feel terrible," I said. "Why live?" I was exaggerating, but if I wasn't going to start dropping ashes on the floor from my bed again I needed to express my emotions.

"Excuse me," Doris said. "I think there's a parent waiting to talk to me." There wasn't. I'd already checked with Judy, the secretary. But I got the message. Get a life.

23

"I've got the flu," Stacey said. A promising sign. I was trying to feel better. I was calling around to find somebody worse off than me and this was my first big break.

"In September?" I said. "It's not even flu season."

"I got it from this woman in the Gold Card division," Stacey said. "Whom I brought out."

"Tough luck," I said happily.

"Did you know if you charge an item on a Gold Card and the item gets lost or stolen within three weeks of purchase, we reimburse you?" she said.

"Not at all," I said. Suddenly I wanted to hang up, bad. For one thing, I hate people who use the first person plural when they're referring to the company they work for. For another, I remembered how tremendously dull Stacey was, especially on the phone. In person, at least she was sort of cute. And, besides all that, what was a forty-year-old woman doing with a name like Stacey?

"Stacey," I said. "I've got to go. A person is waiting for the phone."

"Where are you?" she said. "You can come over. I don't think I'm contagious anymore. I heard you took in a student boarder." Now her voice was becoming sickeningly smooth. I also just remembered that Stacey was extremely prurient.

"Ex-student and she's gone now," I said. "Listen, I should go. I was just checking in. You might try some Chinese herbs."

"You didn't bring her out, did you?" Stacey said.

"Who?" I said. "Oh, Tina. Of course not. What is all this, Stacey? You got bringing out on the brain?"

"No," she said. "I was just thinking about all those high school girls all these years."

"Jeez, Stacey," I said. "You know me better than that." But when I hung up, I realized she probably didn't.

Cars whizzed past the pay phone I was calling from. I'd only gotten a couple of blocks from school when the urge to contact a loser hit so I'd jumped in the first booth I could find. Now I wondered who else to call. Someone less healthy, uglier, less loved, poorer, more hopeless? Someone who wished she was me?

I thought of this computer operator I knew, not an ex-lover, who'd confided in me about her recent brother/sister incest flashbacks, but calling her right now seemed really bankrupt, even to me.

I thought of this Russian studies professor named Helene who had broken up with her longest lover (seven years) a while ago and now loved a woman twenty-five years her junior who insisted the age difference was too big a hurdle. Thus Helene was valiantly dating the shuffling old vegetables (her words) she found listed in the personals section of the local lesbian paper.

Helene actually thought it was funny that I was calling her to feel better because her life was so much worse than mine.

"Oh, well," she said, laughing happily. "At least I'm alive."

I'd told Helene the truth because she had this terrific sense of the absurdity of life. I was counting on her to understand the mess I'd made of mine.

"You like older women and I like ones your age," she said with a chuckle. "Too bad we don't like each other."

"Not in general," I said. "Just that one time with Blaire."

"In general our ugly wrinkled bodies revolt you, is that it?" Helene said. Her tone wasn't quite as fun as it had been a moment before.

"Not at all," I said. "Your bodies aren't ugly and wrinkled, I mean and even if they were . . . ."

"Besides," she said, now quite unkindly, "who says my life is so much worse than yours? What's so much worse? They sound fairly similar when you think about it."

"Okay," I said, giving up.

"I mean," she went on, "you'll be damn lucky to be in my shape in fifteen years."

"You're right," I said.

"At least I love somebody," Helene said, "albeit unrequitedly."

"Absolutely," I said.

"Want to come for dinner?" she said. "I've got two filets thawing."

"No thanks," I said. "I don't want to talk to you anymore, Helene. I'm feeling worse, not better."

"Sorry," she said. But I could tell she wasn't. Now she was happy there was somebody in the world worse off than she was.

Of course there were thousands, maybe millions of people in the world much worse off than either of us but that wasn't the point. It never is. What matters is how the stars and moon look through your particular pair of lenses. Hope helps. In fact, that's probably what it all boils down to. And everybody who doesn't have it might as well just give up.

I didn't have any hope right now at all. I'd used it up on my phone call to Helene.

Late students kept walking by my pay phone, sweaty from sports or excited about things I hoped weren't sex or drugs. Everybody was talking and messing with each other in a chummy way you don't get with most adults, at least in the United States. Adults hardly ever touch each other unless they're lovers. And that last thought made me sad all over again because who notices those things unless they're hopelessly single?

Just then Tina walked by holding hands with the basketball coach and biology teacher, Fred Harris, a hulking bear at least fifteen years her senior.

I was shocked. I knocked on the glass of the phone booth at

them even though I could have just as easily stepped out. Tina saw me and waved Coach Harris on.

"What's the deal, Tina?" I said. We were crammed into the booth together, like Superman and Lois. "Did your mom get you back on track or what?" My face was so close to hers I could practically see through her young, poreless skin. I was actually sneering. I couldn't remember why we were supposed to be friends.

"It's a stage," Tina said. "He's okay."

"You have a thing for teachers?" I said.

"I met him last week when his brakes went out. Amazon was the closest garage he could coast to," Tina said. She was already so bored with me.

"He sure as hell wouldn't have taken his car in there otherwise," I sneered.

"Your nostrils are flaring," she said. "I've never seen them do that before."

"He's balding, Tina," I said. "He's a man."

"Why are you so irrational about men?" she asked me.

"Is it love?" I said.

"I never actually had him as a teacher," she said, "so it's not incestuous or anything."

"But he's a coach," I whined.

"Oh, really," Tina said. "You're getting like an old maid or something. Like you just need a good—"

"Thank you," I said, cutting her off so I wouldn't have to hate her forever.

"I love you anyway," she said, getting the last word, and then she flounced away, leaving me standing there, all impotent, like Clark Kent without his cape.

I decided to call information.

"Information?" I said to the operator.

"For what city?" she said.

"I don't know," I said. "Some city in the Northeast probably."

"You have to tell me what city," the operator said, "so I can connect you to information there."

"I don't want another operator," I said. "I want you to handle it."

"I can't," she said, "but I'll get my supervisor."

"Okay," I said, "you get your supervisor."

"You have to know what city," the supervisor said a moment later, but her tone sounded promising, like maybe she was the kind who enjoyed a challenge at the end of the day.

"I could probably narrow it down to Boston, New Haven and New York," I said.

"Is the last name common?" she said.

"Yes," I said, apologetically. "But the first name isn't."

"Okay," the supervisor said. "It's a deal. You've got yourself a deal."

"But you handle it," I said. "Don't give me to somebody else back east."

"Okay," she said.

"Blaire Bennett," I said. I spelled out the whole name. I was figuring that she'd be a poet-in-residence someplace.

"Hang on," the supervisor said. "I'll get back to you in a minute." And she did. "Jackpot," she said. "Boston, Mass." And then she gave me the number and the street address, too.

"Wait," I said. "Isn't the address against the rules? What if I were a crazy fan wielding a gun? You'd be in big trouble."

"What's she famous for, anyway," the supervisor said, "that you'd be such a fan?"

"She's a poet. She won a Pulitzer a few years back," I said. "But I'm more a friend than a fan."

"Yeah, sure," the supervisor said. "Such a good friend you don't even know where she lives."

"Listen," I said, "I don't have to take this. What's your name?"

"Number 5694," she said.

"Right," I said. "Your first name is 'number'?"

"I'm not supposed to tell you my name," she said. "What if you're a crazy customer?"

"Number 5694, I've only tried to kill one person in my life," I said.

"Okay," she said, laughing because she thought I was joking. "Susanna Broome. I guess one isn't a pattern or anything. Tell me about Blaire Bennett."

"Is this all right?" I said. "Aren't we tying up the phone lines or something?"

"I'm a supervisor, for God's sake," Susanna said.

"I'm not sure if she likes me anymore," I said. "I wanted the option of softening her up epistolarily. By letter."

"I know what epistles are," the supervisor said. "I have a decent education. I hate that."

"I'm sorry," I said and I was. "I just didn't want to sound pretentious."

"Then don't use the word in the first place," Susanna said.

"Wait," I said. "Don't cut me off. You have all the power."

"Yeah," she said, and then she played me a busy signal, a this-number-is-not-in-service-at-this-time, and some other high-pitched buzzing I'd never heard before.

"What's that?" I said.

"We're just trying it out experimentally," she said. "It means 'the number you have dialed is in another area code.' "

"Wow," I said. "That one's pretty intense."

"So you're in love with her or what?" Susanna said.

"Are you a . . . ?" I said.

"Of course," Susanna said. "I know all about Blaire Bennett. 'Signals from a Mountaintop,' 'Curse of a Hero at Large.' I was just playing dumb to feel you out. To see what you were up to."

"I could still be in love with her if she'd let me," I said. "I kind of ran away from her a few months ago. I was afraid she was too much of a good thing." Technically that wasn't the reason at all. She'd cheated on me. But if I was going to call her up, I pretty much had to reframe the whole thing.

"I'm here on most weekdays," Susanna said. "Give me a call if she isn't."

"Isn't what?" I said.

"Interested anymore," she said.

After we hung up I looked at Blaire's phone number over and over again in my little phone booth in the dark. Actually the booth itself was well lighted but I was beginning to feel somewhat vulnerable as night moved in on me. I wondered what Blaire was doing right now in her fabulous town house on Beacon Hill or her funky walk-up in the Italian North End. Was she writing poetry? Was she kissing someone? Was she back with Dale? Would she be glad to hear from me?

I called information again.

"Do you think I should call her, 5694, now?" I said. "I promise I won't bother you again if you just tell me this." Irrationally I was afraid the operator would start treating me mean when she knew I needed her, like everybody else always did.

"Call her," she said.

"Of course you'd say that," I said. "You're the phone company."

24

Blaire answered on the first ring.

"You were just waiting for me to call, weren't you?" I said.

"Who is this?" she said. "Is it you?"

"Yes," I said. "Information gave me your number."

"Well, finally," she said. "I'd almost given up on you."

"I didn't know where you lived," I said. "I'm still mad at you. This phone call is aberrant behavior. It's a full moon."

"I'm so glad you called," Blaire said. "I wasn't done with you."

My heart leaped. Calling Blaire was only asking for trouble but I'd just decided that what else was living for anyway? Safe and solitary wasn't exactly working anymore. If I didn't get a life pretty soon, I'd probably evaporate and blow away.

"Me, either, actually," I said. Then there was a big pause.

"So why'd you run away?" she said.

I couldn't say a thing.

"Never mind," she said.

"You were mean to me. It made sense at the time," I said.

She said, "Did you really try to kill your mother?"

"Yes," I said.

"How?" Blaire said.

"I think you're collecting gory material for your poems," I said. "Is that why you like me? Is this the 'minister's black veil' syndrome?"

"What?" Blaire said.

"Evil turns you on," I said.

"Trying to kill your mother is the last reason I'd like you," Blaire said and she was laughing. "Especially if I'm the new mother figure."

"So are you getting on the next plane or what?" I said, like I'd just forgiven her for Dale and everything else she'd probably do to me in the future. Like all of a sudden I trusted her completely. Like all I wanted was not to be alone.

Of course, I'd forgotten to ask Blaire why she hadn't tried to call me if she wasn't finished with me yet. I was too thrilled that she remembered who I was at all. I felt so good I ran all the way home in the dark and wrote Blaire a letter with a poem in it to seal our bond.

The poem I sent to Blaire

The Breast-Thief

> The woman is running
> Along the edge of a river
> Naked, of course,
> Screaming in a shrill
> Foreign language
> Pressing her breasts to
> Her chest as if they are
> Precious sacks of gold or
> Grain or small babies
>
> The children are running
> Behind her, screaming too
> But you can understand
> That they are saying
> "Stop mama, stop mama
> Give us those breasts"
> And she falls, of course
> And they are upon her
>
> Romulus and Remus
> At each teat

She tries to
Bat them away
But they have teeth
They hang on
Even though those breasts
Have been stone dry
As long as life

Right away, Blaire began to write me letters and send me poems-in-progress. She said she was over her writer's block and she called me her muse. For some reason, she was now also saying she loved me. She was almost a different person. I was like the star of an obscure and enigmatic foreign film and only Blaire owned the script. I read everything she sent, over and over, obsessively. I analyzed every dash for clues.

"God, that's a fine image," Doris said about a line with a woman and a stick and a crow in it.

"I don't get it," I said, wondering only if the poem was about me. I had begun to speculate that the real reason Blaire could send me poems now and love me was because we were still long distance. I was pretty sure once she stepped off the plane, she wouldn't be able to pick me out of the crowd.

I drank more of the coffee Doris poured me while she read on. We were sitting in her kitchen on a Saturday afternoon and Doris was drinking kioki coffee already. I didn't care what she drank as long as we got to talk about Blaire.

Doris explained that the line alluded to a rather famous Chinese fairy tale and made a point about women and internalized victimization.

"Oh," I said.

"God, this is amazing," Doris said, reading another line, this time about matching suitcases being loaded into an airplane.

"I'm not smart enough for her," I said.

"Nonsense," she said. "Besides, Blaire's an artist. She doesn't want brilliance; she wants you to mirror her, to give her back to herself."

"How can I give her back to herself when I don't have the faintest idea what she's talking about?" I said.

"You're exaggerating," Doris said, making herself another drink. Then she sat down and began to read another one of Blaire's poems. In the middle, she laughed out loud.

"Do you love me?" I said. I knew I was being an asshole but I didn't care. I knelt down at her pudgy knees like her new suitor. "Even though I don't get the poetry?" Doris was wearing an oversized Minnie Mouse nightshirt that had slipped up to midthigh. "Do you love me?"

She waved me away from her. "Read me some more," she said.

"I shouldn't," I said falsely. It seemed kind of indelicate not to hesitate. But then I sat back down in my black director's chair and pulled another letter out of my bag.

Part of Blaire's letter to me

I want to meet your cats and your friends. I want to watch you work and take a bath with you by candlelight. I want to watch your eyelids move while you sleep.

"That's enough," Doris said. "I get the idea."

"There's more," I said.

"Fine," Doris said. "But that's enough. I meant poems."

"Maybe you'll find love again," I said, blissfully misunderstanding her reaction the way those in love always do.

"I don't want love again," she said. "Read my lips."

"Oh, Doris," I cooed and put my arm around her shoulders. She squirmed out and said, "Stop it."

"I don't understand you," I said. "Love is everything. It's at the base of everything."

"You are so silly," she said.

I looked her in the face and suddenly I knew she was right. What I didn't understand was: if love wasn't everything, what was?

25

While I waited the month for Blaire to come visit me, I bought travel magazines and imagined us there, leaning over a white marble balcony on a blue bay in Corfu, or lying across a huge sleigh bed in a Norwegian ski lodge, or sunbathing naked on a flat rock in the middle of a lake in Switzerland. I read decorating journals and cradled us in woody living rooms, in sultry bedrooms, in bathrooms surrounded by clouds.

Ah, I was full. Trees seemed taller, grass seemed greener, food tasted richer. Certainly masturbation had never been so rewarding. Blaire was with me; my hand was her hand, my lips were kissing hers. No longer was self-stimulation a lonely, vaguely embarrassing occupation. It was my spiritual bridge to Blaire, my lifeline and a real release. Sometimes when I read her letters I'd get so excited I didn't know what else to do except lie down on my bed and make myself come.

It was almost as if things were better with Blaire because of the bad stuff that had happened in New Mexico. We were getting a second chance and this time we'd do it right. Still, in my fantasies, we were so deeply and completely and safely in love that I almost didn't want her to get here at all.

26

A week after I'd seen her with Coach, Tina invited herself over for a visit. She was bearing several sweet little cartons of delicately spiced Thai food like a ritual offering of appeasement to me, the angry goddess of sexual orientation. I put the cartons on the coffee table and we spooned the contents out onto our plates. Coconut milk, peanut oil, hot peppers, pineapple, noodles, chicken, cashews, lemon root, and shrimp swam around in fragrant circles on our plates.

"The smells," I said, practically fainting.

"Are you still mad at me?" she said.

"No," I said, picking up some Pad Thai noodles with my splintery take-out chopsticks. "You've appeased me completely."

"Doris told me that you're in love with Blaire again," Tina said as if that explained everything. "Kind of takes the edge off, doesn't it?"

"Off of what?" I said.

"Troubles, worries, whatever," Tina said.

"How would you know?" I said. "Not with Coach?"

"Fred," Tina said.

"I haven't trusted a straight woman in ten years, Tina," I said.

"You said you weren't angry anymore," she said.

"I'm not," I said. "I just don't trust you." And then I took another big helping of all the food and ate it as slowly as I could.

"I'm bisexual, not straight," Tina said finally.

"So I can half trust you? It doesn't work that way," I said, in spite of the sparkling tears rising around the corners of her eyes. Weeping didn't humanize her one bit. "Bisexuals are worse than straights," I said.

Suddenly she sat up and wiped her eyes.

"There are a million things more important than the number of x chromosomes your lover has," she said. "Homelessness, politics, our fascist government, to name a few."

"Did Coach teach you that?" I said.

"Doris is straight," Tina said. "And you trust her."

"Doris is nothing," I said. "She's sexless. Neuter."

I was getting a little bored with this line of discussion but I wanted Tina to know what the stakes were in life. I wanted her to know she couldn't have everything. That you're always having to give up one thing or another.

"I never expected you to be this rigid," she said.

"You can't have it both ways," I said.

"What?" Tina said.

"You can't love a man and have lesbians fall all over themselves to get close to you. Come on," I said. That much was clear to me. What wasn't clear was why I was being hard on the poor kid who was still so young she barely had a driver's license. Why did I care so much who the hell she slept with?

"Oh, jeez," she said.

And then all of a sudden I knew why I was being this way, so exaggerated and humorless. Hadn't my mother left me and my father for man after man after man?

"It's okay," I said. "I got lost in my unhappy childhood." I didn't need to tell Tina she was playing my mother and Coach wasn't Coach at all. "I overreacted."

"I guess so," Tina said. "Anyway, I wanted to tell you that I'm going to move in with Fred this month."

"Swell," I said. "Don't you want Piston back?" Piston was almost grown up now and spent most of her time hanging around the bird feeder in the backyard like a teenage hood.

"This is totally her place now," she said. "Besides, Fred has an Afghan hound."

After she went home I put everything that was left in all the cartons into the biggest one of them, layering the different flavors as carefully as I could. I was happy I had lunch for tomorrow taken care of and no dinner dishes at all.

I let Tina go. I didn't need her anymore. I had Blaire.

Then there was some television program on about this woman who was having a singularly dreary extramarital love affair. After her paraplegic husband drowned himself in the backyard swimming pool I turned it off even though I had a feeling his suicide didn't resolve a thing. It made me think about my mother.

I hadn't actually ever seen her in the act. Thank God. All I knew is that while she was married to my father she slept with a lot of other men. Why? For the hell of it, I guess. Because they were there.

I knew about how sexy my mother was because one night a few years before I tried to kill her, she'd bragged about it over dinner. Here she was into her third marriage and probably she'd finally noticed that I'd hardly ever had anybody myself. I'd specially prepared sweetbreads and rice in a cream sauce for her birthday but she didn't eat much.

Instead, she drank wine and told me her adventures. But she wouldn't tell me the names of her male lovers. She'd been with a couple of women and she told me who they were, but the men's names were off-limits.

"Why?" I'd asked her.

"Because some of them were married," she'd said. This seemed to make perfect sense to her although I knew for a fact that the women she'd slept with were married too. And this indication of how to her women sleeping together didn't matter, when she knew perfectly well that I was a lesbian, wasn't it just one more good reason for me to drive her into that tree a couple years later?

27

The next day, during my prep period, my new favorite student, Ashley, came to me to tell me that she thought she might be pregnant, that she had turned to me of all the teachers because she was so certain that I'd understand best. Ashley was real average looking except for her intense brown eyes. She was also terrifically smart and never did her schoolwork, on principle, it seemed.

"I have absolutely no ambition, but that doesn't mean I want to have a kid at seventeen, much less raise one," she said.

I looked at her and tried to focus on her problem but mostly I was trying to imagine her enjoying heterosexual sex with some adolescent boy. And I was trying to figure out what she wanted me of all people to do about it.

"I like underachievers, Ashley," I said. "I really do. I'm one myself, actually, and I agree that tendency shouldn't sentence you to a crummy life. On the other hand, I can't really tell you what to do. You go home and think about your options and if you want to, come back and tell me your decision."

"Any books I ought to read?" she said.

"Why?" I said. "You won't read them. You never read them."

"At least give me a chance to reject it," she said, which was probably the point.

"All right Ashley," I said. "Try *Tess of the d'Urbervilles*. There's a vague similarity to your situation even though it's English, nineteenth century."

"My situation is sort of timeless, isn't it?" Ashley said. "What a jerk I am."

"It's a long book," I said. "It might take you the full nine months to get through it."

When she left I realized that silly remark probably had more impact than several weeks of pregnancy counseling.

No one can deny that *To the Lighthouse* is a stupid choice of a novel for high school students no matter how smart they are. Not one girl has ever recognized any of the emotional threads running between the characters or within Lucy or Mrs. Ramsay. What healthy, strapping girl of seventeen is capable of reflecting on Lucy's need for mother love and artistic courage? What happening girl in the nineties is going to be concerned with Mrs. Ramsay's compulsive need to take care of others, much less the inner life of an empty beach house?

In their essays, the very clever ones spread out these ideas and then wove them together in a cold tapestry of literary analysis brimming with quoted support and supple transitions. But the writing was so sad because there was no identification underneath holding it all together. A case could be made that reinforcing this nimble sleight-of-hand was worse than not reading the book at all because of what it taught—that staying on the surface is what education is all about.

But I didn't care about that. Not really. I continued to teach *To the Lighthouse* every year because I loved to read it and I loved to hear myself talk about it even if the faces in front of me were as blank as the driven snow. I blocked them out and stepped inside the book again, usually as the shamelessly honest Lily Briscoe, locked in perpetual struggle to capture Mrs. Ramsay forever in the middle of her canvas.

So, two days before Blaire was scheduled to arrive, after dinner, I read three or four essays and promised myself once more that I would never desecrate the book again by putting it into the Neanderthal hands of a seventeen-year-old. But I gave the

competent ones high marks anyway because, of course, i.
best they could do.

Finally, I picked up the last essay. Paper-clipped to the top was
a cryptic note from Ashley. It said—"I thought about my problem overnight and decided that *Tess* is way too long. Do you
think it's a sin?"

On the top of her essay I wrote—"No, Ashley. It's not a sin. It's
just a difficult decision." And then I gave her essay on *To the
Lighthouse* a B+ for the sophistication of her writing style. I'm
positive she never opened that book either.

Then I put the essays away in my notebook and thought about
what a good teacher I was and what a fine mother I would have
been even though I had absolutely no model for it at all. And
that made me wonder why some people like me overcome the
way they were raised and some people like my mother just per-
petuate it. Then, because the answer—some people are good
and some people are bad—was too simplistic even for me, I went
back to Virginia Woolf, the sacred source of mother knowledge
herself.

I picked up the book, my personal first edition which cost
$125 at a cozy bookstore up the coast. The cover, on which Va-
nessa had drawn a whimsical bunch of abstract flowers bordering
title and author, was still delightfully intact. I turned to my favorite page; I kept a blue satin string in the book for easy reference,
and read out loud.

My *favorite passage*

From To the Lighthouse

Sitting on the floor with her arms round Mrs. Ramsay's
knees, close as she could get, smiling to think that Mrs.
Ramsay would never know the reason of that pressure, she
imagined how in the chambers of the mind and heart of
the woman who was, physically, touching her, were stood,
like the treasures in the tombs of kings, tablets bearing sacred inscriptions, which if one could spell them out,
would teach one everything but they would never be of-

fered openly, never made public. What art was there, known to love or cunning, by which one pressed through into those secret chambers? What device for becoming, like waters poured into one jar, inextricably the same, one with the object one adored? Could loving, as people called it, make her and Mrs. Ramsay one?

Then, in spite of the warm recognition circling around and through my heart, the ever new pleasure in the sense that somebody else knew the feelings for women I kept hidden, for shame, I began to remember more about my own mother, that hero of my childhood, that river leech who had worked her way so far inside my skin that I'd tried to kill her to get her out.

I took out my journal and began to write. I wanted to contain my inner life on paper, in words, like I'd tried to do in my cold and steely poems at Taos. Fat chance.

My journal entry

Why she hated me I'll never know. But I know it was real. It was the only real thing between us.

I tried to change the subject but of course it was way too late. I was sitting on a raft and it was going downstream whether I liked it or not.

I closed the journal.

I had dreams about sex with my mother. That was another secret. No one in the world knew it and there were no books like *To the Lighthouse* where a charming and artistic Lily admitted and transformed a secret like mine. In my dream I wanted my mother so badly I was rolling on her like she was a dead thing and I was a wolfhound consumed by the smell. I rubbed her breasts between my legs and I tasted her wetness with my tongue. She never touched me. The dream always ended abruptly when we were interrupted by someone far more thrilling than I ever could be.

And now, just like those three women at the writers' conference and just like my last girlfriend, I started remembering things my mother used to do to me, that I'd forgotten until now, as Blaire Bennett was about to arrive to be my brand new love.

I saw hands. My mother's hands touching me between my legs, putting cream on my vulva. Her hands between her own legs in my bed late at night. Her hands hitting me, pushing me, covering my mouth. I saw those things until I couldn't look anymore and then I lay back in my chair, closed my eyes and breathed.

I listened to the sounds in my house. Amanda scratching around in the kitty litter, the refrigerator humming, the windy groaning of the traffic on the freeway not too far away. My mother used to come into my room late at night to cover me with my blanket or check on my open window. Then she used to climb into my bed and rub my flat breasts to make them grow. She put her finger up inside me to make me big, to make me wet. I never opened my eyes. I tried to be asleep.

I let a long time go by before I moved so it could all sink in and I could come back to being me, now. I cried some too, because of how horrible and disgusting the memories were. And because it felt like the things were all happening to me again.

But, when I finally got up to eat dinner, I didn't feel so terrible anymore. I felt sort of peaceful and relieved because of things finally making sense. I still didn't have the answer to why my mother had been so bad to me but at least I knew I wasn't crazy. It was okay now to hate her. And it was okay that I wanted her dead.

28

After work I drove to my mother's house with a gun in the glove compartment of my car. The school bookkeeper had loaned it to me to protect myself after I told her all about the explosive temper of my boyfriend whom I was still trying to leave. Everybody was always borrowing Nicki's gun and then returning it a few days later, unfired. All you had to do was tell her a long, sad, very personal story that required a gun and, plunk, there it was on your lap.

One reason, we speculated, she was so generous was that she must have been desperate to have visitors. She was probably terribly lonely in her office which was in a completely separate building from everybody else's. Another reason was that she was bored being a bookkeeper. What Nicki did when we weren't visiting her and she wasn't busy with ledgers and things was read fat gothic romances and watch her favorite soap opera on the tiny portable TV she kept hidden inside the file drawer. Nicki was our secret; nobody had ever told Doris a thing.

The deal was you had to promise her that you'd return the gun and then you had to tell her a whole new story about what you did with it. Everybody always said they'd fired it and wounded their enemy, but not critically.

"Ah." She'd sit back, folding her hands across her big stomach. "Good work."

Most people gave her a large box of Godiva truffles when they returned the gun. It was the least we could do.

So here I was with the gun in my very own glove compartment. It was small and pearl handled, cradled on an orange chamois which Nicki always threw in for concealment purposes. This was the first time I'd ever borrowed it and I kept thinking it would go off every time I hit a speed bump. There were a lot of them crossing the balmy golf paths of my mother's gated and exclusive community.

After convincing the guard that my mother had certainly intended to give me a guest pass, I parked a ways down the street from her house. All I could see of it was a garage and a wall with a large black door in the middle of it. My mother lived in a fortress of gray brick. How pleased she must have been. How safe she was. From the entire world and me.

It was twilight now. The streetlights in this brand new golfing community were made to look like gaslights in the French Quarter, the gatehouse looked like a diminutive Monticello, the clubhouse looked like a huge trappers' lodge in the Pacific Northwest. New was bad but old was bad too. It was only okay if something obviously brand new emulated something old. Everything in this place was a lie and a scam.

I reached into the glove compartment and touched the gun. I knew Nicki probably wouldn't like it if I actually did shoot, not just in my imagination, but what choice did I have? My mother was making me mad again.

The first time I tried to kill her, my mother had simply been talking about herself, about a vacation she was going to take with her new husband, to Death Valley, for some reason her favorite place on earth. She was talking about the grand hotel there, the remarkable food, the salt crystal creeks and the moonlight hikes. When she moved to look at me her eyes were so smoky and glazed I knew that for an instant she had no idea who on earth she was talking to. That's when I turned the wheel toward the tree. At that moment I knew it was either her or me. There was only world enough for one of us at a time.

The thing now was that thinking about where I was going to

put the bullet and what she'd look like when she fell to the ground was getting me almost too excited to shoot straight. I'd only fired a gun a couple of times before, once at a shooting range with this tremendous butch named Barb and once at the country fair where the guns don't actually use bullets but send laser messages or something. I'd done okay both times but I wasn't a natural mark or anything like that. I certainly couldn't afford to be shaking when I aimed at my mother.

I needed a drink or a Valium, neither of which I'd thought to bring with me. So, instead, I unzipped my pants and pulled them down to my knees. I put my jacket over my lap and touched myself with fast and twitchy strokes until I had an orgasm. Then I pulled my pants up, leaned back in my seat and watched the streetlights come on. Masturbating had calmed me down enough to shoot straight but now I didn't care all that much about making my mother die either. At least for tonight.

Besides, it was starting to rain and I hated driving on the freeway in a storm. And, besides that, just as I was beginning to think about turning on the engine and the lights and the windshield wipers, the garage door opened and extruded a convertible beige Rolls-Royce Corniche, license plate PUTT PUT, probably to commemorate the golfing hobby of my mother and her present husband and to charm the freeway Marxists who would have enjoyed nothing better than to sideswipe them right off the road.

The top was up because of the rain but I could see that my mother was in the driver's seat. I stared at her deeply but it didn't help. All I could see was on the surface. She looked almost as handsome and young as she had ten years before but nothing about her explained what made her so mean. The man sitting beside her, evidently Martin, stepfather number three, looked dangerously antique, crepey and translucent almost, under the early evening streetlights. Which didn't surprise me. My mother's partners never matched her at all.

29

The next day, when Blaire arrived, I didn't tell her that I'd almost killed my mother again. A failed attempt ten years ago was romantic and stimulating. A day ago she'd probably think certifiably mad. And because I really didn't feel like telling her all about my recent flashbacks as support, I wouldn't blame her if she did.

"You tried to kill your mother again, didn't you?" Blaire said anyway.

"You look swell," I said. She did. Her white hair was cut in a snappy brush cut and she seemed so glad to see me I let myself believe it.

"You did," Blaire said.

"You are very prescient," I said. "That must be why you're such a great poet." At this, I shivered slightly. I kept forgetting how important and famous she was at times like this. Times when we were talking about me.

"Look at me," she said. "I'm not laughing." It was a little tough to see her face because I was driving but from the side I could tell that she wasn't even smiling. She was wearing a white linen jacket and pants and carrying a bunch of calla lilies which some fan had given her at the airport.

"You look hard and soft at the same time," I said.

"There's something nerved up about you," she said. "You're all pink."

"I didn't actually try to kill her. I sat in my car outside her house holding a gun I'd borrowed from work," I said. "That's all I did."

"They loan out guns at work?" Blaire said.

"Sure," I said. "We're just not supposed to shoot them."

"I love you," Blaire said.

"Why do you?" I said.

"I already told you at the workshop," she said.

"No you didn't," I said. "You told me you couldn't love anybody but if you could it probably would be me and then you said it was because I gave everything I had."

"Good memory," she said.

"It's important," I said. "Why do you?"

"Maybe you taught me how," Blaire said. "People change."

"You're so much nicer," I said, "than you used to be. At the workshop you had a fast mouth."

She smiled at me but she didn't say a thing. Finally she said, "Maybe because this isn't as much of a game anymore. With you."

Nothing Blaire was telling me made any sense at all but I wanted to be with her so much I didn't care. Why was she here? Was she looking for a warmer climate to pass the frigid semester off? Were her other prospects not working out? Was she some sort of sadist voyeur?

I said, "She's going to take you away from me."

"Your mother?" she said. "I don't even know her."

"It's more complicated than that," I said. "It's too much for right now. It's something really bad."

"I know what it is already," she said. "You don't have to tell me."

Maybe she had powers of the occult. Maybe she could read my mind.

"No you don't, Blaire," I said. "Trust me."

Then she did a dangerous thing. At the next stoplight, she unfastened her seatbelt, moved over, put her hand on my cheek and kissed my mouth tremendously. Then she said, "Forget Mom. This is Blaire."

30

I tried to, I honestly did. I made love to Blaire three times a day. I took her to all my favorite places: the rocky waterfall at the end of a steep trail, the flagstone patio where they served coffee and cake, the freeway on-ramp that curved into the sky at night. I showed her where I shopped for groceries, my library, and the gay video store. I took her to see my classroom, the house where I was conceived and the gravestones of one set of grandparents. The trouble was that the closer I got to Blaire the more room I needed inside me for the two of us to live in. The more I needed to get rid of my mother. She was taking up too much space all over again.

One night we went to a difficult play about childhood sexual abuse.

"That was fun," Blaire said dryly, when the incest play was over and we were driving home.

"At least there was music and slides of children running through fields of flowers," I said. "And that famous actress who introduced it was nice. I bet it happened to her." And then I pulled the car over into a loading zone and opened the door because I thought I was going to be sick.

"What's happening?" Blaire said.

"I need to throw up," I said and then I took a couple of deep breaths. "It's from someplace deeper than my stomach," I said. And then, almost immediately, I felt better. I closed the door and looked at Blaire. "The last girlfriend who left me was an incest survivor and I used to have to listen to all her flashbacks and everything."

"Oh," Blaire said, like that was it.

"But now I have to listen to mine," I said.

"I thought so," she said.

"You did?" I said.

"I could see it in your eyes the first time we made love," she said. "Like something else was happening besides me."

"I can take you back to the airport if you're not into this," I said, which was a big deal for me. Because of what it implied. That she might want to stay.

She did.

We sat in the car and I looked straight ahead and talked.

"I used to think she was taking extra-specially good care of me. When the area around my vagina would get sore she'd put Vaseline on it."

Blaire touched my face briefly, with her knuckles.

"She had me play with her breasts," I said. "Sometimes I'd tell her that my vulva hurt when it didn't. So she would put Vaseline on it.

"I'd push her breasts around like punching bags," I said. "They were big."

There were actually tears in Blaire's eyes. I looked at her for a long time. I'd never seen that before. It was like a miracle to have somebody else cry about my own sad story.

"When I was ten or eleven she used to get in bed with me at night. I'd pretend to be asleep," I said.

"Once in a while she'd get on top of me, but mostly she'd lie next to me and rub herself with her hand," I said.

Now I watched the streetlights change from green to yellow to red over and over and over. It was pleasant and comforting, like they were an inevitable part of the natural cycle, not just technology.

"What I still don't get is why she hates me so much," I said.

Blaire didn't try to do anything like hold my hand or patch me up. She was looking straight ahead at the lights too.

"I think I'm done," I said. "For now. Just tell me it wasn't my fault."

Blaire took my hand in hers and pressed it hard. "It wasn't your fault," she said. "It was hers."

I closed my eyes and leaned into Blaire's arms. I was so glad she was with me I couldn't say another word. I listened to her heart beating and thought about how this was just like my dreams and my fantasies that had never happened in real life. I wanted to climb inside her so that it would never end.

"I could die right now, happily," I said. "I mean because I'm so happy."

She began to rock me, just a little bit.

"Never hurt me," I said.

"No," she said. "I never will."

I might have been done then but Blaire wasn't. We drove to my favorite patio place for coffee and once we got there she had a lot to say. She was one of these take-action people about bad things. She wanted us to invite my mother over to lunch and then confront her about the sexual stuff. I said I'd rather just try to kill her again.

Blaire won, I guess. I agreed that I would invite my mother to lunch and that I would confront her with what she'd done to me. I insisted that Blaire had to come along to help me out. What I didn't know then was that when she and my mother met each other at the doorway of the chic pine and linen restaurant named Sleigh, they'd fall in love.

Well, if not in love exactly, they did make a pretty pair. They were both attractive in a sort of rugged way, although my mother tried to soften it up with makeup and femmy accessories. I was so much younger, like the kid, that I almost wasn't in the equation at all. Some heavy-duty energy was flowing between them that made me sick. When they walked in, everybody in the room stared. I trailed behind them, a queasy mouse, that nobody noticed at all.

"Darling," my mother said, turning to me. "It's been too long. I'm so pleased that you got in touch with me at last." She wasn't glad to see me in the least and we both knew it. She was onstage now and everything was for the benefit of Blaire.

"Blaire Bennett," my mother said, after we sat down. "I've read your work."

"You remind me of someone," Blaire said. And this time she meant it. Me, except my mother was the original ore. I was only the plated copy.

"Let's have champagne," my mother said. "I love your suit." Blaire was wearing a suede pants suit with a creamy silk blouse.

"Yours is very nice as well," Blaire said. "May I?" And she actually took a pinch of my mother's Chinese silk jacket between her fingers.

I pushed my chair back and looked at both of them. I tried to see them as the silly subjects in a hyper-realist painting satirizing ladies who lunch. But then I realized that it was me who was the joke. It was finally completely obvious that everything rotten in the universe was using me as its hub.

"Where do you find friends like this?" My mother laughed at me.

"In hell," I said. "At the bottom of the La Brea Tar Pits with the dying mastodons." But nobody was listening. My mother was already back at work on Blaire.

"It's so wonderful to meet you, Blaire," my mother said, reaching for her hand over the dozen bluepoint oysters we were supposed to share. "And to see you too, dear," she said to me, reaching for my hand too. It was a complicated gesture but it worked, for her.

In more ways than one.

I couldn't speak.

And Blaire was disarmed, or something.

She and my mother discussed poetry and life on the eastern seaboard and fine couture while I ate three more appetizers, a chef's salad, pasta in pernod and cream, half a loaf of sourdough and a piece of praline cheesecake.

Nobody spoke to me.

And nobody mentioned incest, abuse or murder.

I watched the charming laugh lines around my mother's mouth, her eyes open wide as she listened to every word Blaire said, as she questioned and flattered her. As her stockinged foot rubbed against Blaire's ankle under the table, as she fed Blaire an oyster from her very own fingers.

I was lying on my back underwater, floating, watching the two of them above the surface, like wavy trees against the blue sky. I was almost drowning.

After an hour and a half, I excused myself and walked six miles home. When I got there the phone rang a lot but I didn't answer it. I went to bed instead.

I put a pillow over my face and blamed myself. I let all four cats sleep on the bed with me so I wouldn't fall off. And then I started shaking.

I didn't really want to go crazy. But Blaire couldn't have done anything worse if she'd tried. She'd gotten me to trust her with my life and then she'd hauled off and broken my heart. Now I had two bad mothers and nothing else inside to show for myself. I hadn't even learned a good lesson except what I knew already. That you give people too big of an opening and all they want to do is ruin your life.

Later, in the dusky light, Blaire sat down on the edge of my bed and rubbed my back under the blanket.

"I should be crying but I can't," I said, into my pillow. "I should cry when something this bad happens."

"She's hypnotizing," Blaire said. "She's dangerous. I forgot why we were there."

"I still love you," I said, "even though you just betrayed the hell out of me."

"She tried to rub my foot under the table," Blaire said. "I didn't eat any lunch. I think she wanted to make love."

"And I've lost all my killer energy," I said. "Now I only want to kill myself."

Blaire didn't hear me. She was in too much trouble herself. I don't think she knew she could do something this bad.

She kept opening and closing her mouth with no words coming out. Then she said, "I've never felt this ashamed before. I want to dig a big hole in the ground and bury myself alive."

More than anything, I wanted her to be the victim, the sister of my soul, not a perpetrator herself. I wanted us to have one more chance.

"It's okay," I said. "Now you understand what she's like."

"Next time I'll help you kill her," Blaire said.

And then, what a miracle, we both started to laugh.

"Now I understand," Blaire said back to me later, before we fell asleep that night. We were wound up all around each other like vines climbing a tree trunk. We were breathing in unison. "And you look exactly like her, twenty years younger."

"She named me after herself," I said. "Down to the middle initial. And now she owns both of us."

"No she doesn't," Blaire said. "We'll just have to try the confrontation over again. But this time I won't look at her directly. I'll use mirrors."

Blaire started falling asleep and I couldn't seem to do anything except lie there and watch her. Her feet kicked and her fingers twitched against my arm. Her lips moved liked she was talking to somebody in her dreams.

"When are you going to break my heart?" I whispered to her soft cheek. "Why do you keep acting like it's love?"

She didn't answer. She was in another world.

"And why do I keep giving you everything I've got?"

She only sighed in her sleep but I got the message just the same. My chest started to ache like both lungs had collapsed. I faced it that Blaire had already broken my heart twice and still I kept on loving her because I needed her so much. That all people do is break each other's hearts and forgive each other, over and over again until one of them can't muster the enthusiasm anymore.

"I still love you, Blaire," I said to her soft cheek. "But not as much as I used to, not as much as I could."

31

We decided not to risk confrontation with my mother again. Instead, this time we decided to go in for some slow torture.

It was fun, at first, making elaborate plans. We could feel some of the release of doing sadistic stuff to my mother without actually lifting a finger. Generally speaking, our intention was to run her through an endless maze of horrors or make her walk a frayed tightrope in a madhouse circus. We wanted to star her in an early David Lynch film.

Blaire and I stopped making love altogether to have time to watch rented videos which were supposed to give us big colorful ideas and put us in the prankster mood.

I particularly liked *The Hunger* with Catherine Deneuve in her smoky drawing room slitting peoples' throats with an Egyptian dagger ankh and then sucking their veins dry.

"Brilliant casting," Blaire agreed as I put the tape on pause to better appreciate the blood dripping from Deneuve's porcelain jaw. "But don't get any ideas. We're twisted jokers and tricksters, not vampires and killers. We're the weird family in *Eraserhead*, not Freddy in *The Nightmare on Elm Street II*.

"Good sex scene too," I said later about Catherine kissing Susan Sarandon's breasts. "It looks like they're enjoying it."

"It looks like they're acting," Blaire said. "We do it a hundred times better, when we do it."

"We'll do it," I said, kissing her neck a little bit. I didn't want to tease her but I did want to be affectionate.

"You, me, Doris, Tina," Blaire said. "What do you think? You got anybody else?"

"For sex?" I said, making a stupid joke.

"To help with the torture," she said, like I was so slow.

"I was thinking just you and me. It's kind of a personal issue," I said.

"They love you," Blaire said. "The more the merrier and the better we'll be. Think Robin Hood. Think merry women."

"They don't actually know about the incest component," I said, "of the motivation. Am I supposed to sit down and explicate that for them?"

"Yeah," Blaire said. I figured she had other healthy reasons for dragging Tina and Doris into it, but for the moment I let her keep them to herself. I wanted Blaire mostly to have things her way because of all the other crap she had to put up with in terms of me.

Still, I had to ask, "But what's in it for you?"

"Your mental health, of course," she said.

She took my hand. "Believe me?" she said.

"Absolutely," I said.

She liked that. She gripped my hand tight, so tight it hurt.

When Doris came over to take back Nicki's gun the next day, I figured, what the hell, get it over with.

She said, "I heard about the gun."

She'd heard about the gun from Nicki no doubt because I still hadn't given it back. I was way over the unspoken time limit and Nicki had probably freaked.

"What gun?" I said. "Who cares about that?"

"Hi, Blaire," Doris said.

"Hi, Doris," Blaire said and then they shook hands across me.

"Sit down, Doris," I said. She didn't look so great but I didn't say anything about it in front of Blaire. Her hair was flat on top and it stuck out straight on the sides. And her face was flushed and fat.

"I know my hair's a mess," Doris said.

"So you finally found out," I said. "People have been borrowing Nicki's gun for years."

"I've known about it for years," she said. "You're the only one I ever worried about."

"I didn't use it," I said.

"Nicki wants it back," Doris said. "Now." Then she lit a cigarette and blew smoke out of her mouth and nose at the same time. "You were going after your mother again."

"You know about the first time?" I said.

"Tina told me," Doris said. "On the trip back from summer camp. While you were pumping gas."

"She must have told it fast," I said.

"What's so long about it?" she said. "You tried to kill your mother ten years ago by driving both of you into a tree. It was a two-minute tale, my dear. No big deal."

I couldn't seem to sit up anymore. Suddenly I was all bent over and talking into my hands.

"What?" Doris said.

Blaire did it for me. She told Doris some of the difficult things that I had told her and also about my mother and Blaire at lunch.

Doris hit the table, hard, with her fist.

Something in the bowels of the house moved. I jumped up to take flight.

"Sit down," Blaire said. "It's okay."

"Something just shifted," I said. "Did you feel it? In the foundation or the walls or someplace."

"No it didn't," Doris said, lifting a frightened cat off her lap.

"Then why is the cat scared?" I said.

"Because Doris hit the table," Blaire said. "Because she was angry at your mother."

Doris looked at her funny like Blaire was in trouble too.

"Blaire couldn't help it," I said. "My mother is impossibly seductive."

"Are you okay?" Doris said.

"Oh," I said. "I go a little bit crazy, I think, with all this public group discussion. It's like I'm standing on the scaffold with Dimmesdale or something."

"What?" Doris said.

"The Scarlet Letter," Blaire said, looking at me happily, as if I couldn't be that upset if I was making dumb literary allusions to Hawthorne again.

"So what now?" Doris said. "Where's Tina?"

"She's fucking Coach," I said.

"You're kidding," she said.

"Who cares?" I said. "Tina only pretended to have depth. Just like everybody I fall for."

"Present company excluded, I presume," said Blaire.

Doris said, "I'm hungry. Got any cheese or pepperoni? Even Velveeta on crackers."

Blaire got us drinks and food. It was all so nice and cuddly it was dangerous. At least for a few minutes, being with them was like I was floating in warm amniotic fluid and I was never again going to have to come up for air.

32

But then they made me re-bond with Tina because it had to be the four of us. So that was the end of that.

It was easy to find her the next day. She was working part-time for Coach as assistant coach—volleyball. I'd heard she worked at Amazon from eight until twelve and then on the courts all afternoon. Saving up money for college, probably.

"Typical," I said to her in the stinky girls' locker room right before she had to go to practice. She was pulling up gladiator knee pads and shin guards and tossing volleyballs into a huge mesh bag. It was like extreme combat she was going off to, not girls' after-school recreation.

"Oh, hi," she said. "I was going to come see you but I didn't know if I was welcome."

"You are so Coach's girl," I said, which wasn't the way to start to bond, exactly, but I wasn't going to let Blaire and Doris run everything. I could at least do it my own way. In my own time.

"You are so Blaire's," Tina said.

"Whoa," I said. She was way out of her league.

"Coach and I are just friends now," she said.

"Too young for him, huh?" I said.

"No," she said. "I broke it off actually."

It figured. Nothing was too young for dumb jocks like Fred.

"You weren't happy then?" I asked her. "With Coach." I tried to hide the hopeful lilt in my voice but things were definitely looking up. So much for men, maybe. My assignment from Blaire and Doris wasn't going to be as difficult to fulfill as I'd thought.

"Even though he was lots older, I kept thinking of him as a brother," she said, "which wasn't too sexy. Sometimes it even got really boring to tell you the truth. Unless you're into incest, I guess." She paused there to tie the shoelace on her right high-top.

"That's kind of what I came over to talk to you about," I said. "But it can wait until after practice."

"You watch then," Tina said. "The team will love it. They'll show off for you. Especially old Ashley, your new fave."

I was pleased that Ashley had taken care of her pregnancy so quickly but I was startled all the same. How good could jumping for spikes be for her recently battered uterus?

"Well?" Tina said.

"Okay," I said. "I'll watch."

Then we walked down to the volleyball courts. I was carrying the huge bag of balls like now I was Tina's assistant and I was smiling because this idea of intense girl sports on sunny after-noons was turning out to be so great.

"He said some good things," Tina said. "Coach did."

"He's not bad," I said.

"He said stuff about how we all need our dreams and nobody can buy you if you don't let them," she said. "He's been in jail, actually, for civil disobedience."

When we arrived at the volleyball courts I waved to Ashley while Tina threw out the balls and organized drills. When she came back to me, she said, "You still like me best, don't you?"

"Best?" I said.

"Better than Ashley?" Tina said.

"Yes," I said. And I put an arm around her shoulders. "We're bonded, baby," I said. "It's for life."

"I don't mean to be pushy but I sort of need it from you to be unconditional," Tina said, "if that's possible."

I was definitely moved, now that it was official. Tina was asking me to be her other mother, her lesbian one.

"I'll try," I said. "It's the best I can do."

It made her so happy to hear me say that I didn't have the heart to tell her what was really on my mind. That unconditional was definitely a thing of the past.

"The point is, as I see it," said Blaire, later that evening at my house, "to publicly ridicule and humiliate the woman. To reduce her to the sniveling worm she truly is."

"I think the point is about scaring her to death," Doris said. "I'd like to see us bury her alive in a pine box and then dig her out ten seconds before she suffocates." She inhaled deeply on her cigarette and smiled. "Five seconds," she said. "That would teach her something."

"Ha," I said. "What?"

"Let's force her to ingest enormous amounts of food," Tina said. "Chili from tin cans, gallons of rocky road ice cream, an entire pink sheetcake from the supermarket, pots of hot oatmeal, thirty buckwheat pancakes, raw hot dogs, pickled herring, a pitcher of Tang."

See what fun we were having?

"How do you remember Tang, Tina?" Blaire said.

"From TV reruns on cable," Tina said. "Sometimes they show old commercials too. Want to see?" She grabbed the remote control and began switching channels. It was annoying but it helped me remember that she was still a kid.

Poor Tina. I'd really made her pay for my unconditional love. She had to hear the shortened, but still sickening, version of why I hated my mother, in that smelly locker room after volleyball practice and then she had to agree to help me out. I felt bad about it but not that bad. She was young but here I was handing her the sadistic adventure of a lifetime, guilt- and risk-free.

"What about you?" Doris said to me.

I said, "Well, I wouldn't mind watching her get gang-raped at knifepoint on CBS news."

"Oh come on," Tina said. She turned off the television. I wasn't being that funny. I was changing the tone.

"Okay," I said. "How about she has to be really poor? And live with chronic back pain somewhere hot and humid with lots of bugs?"

"Not bad," Blaire said.

"Am I doing better?" I said. I knew I was because Blaire had begun to rub my foot.

"We aren't really going to act on this, are we?" I said.

"Listen, baby," Doris said. "This is nothing. You were about to murder her."

"Yes, but . . ." I said. Now I was thinking that Blaire's reason for getting us to do this together was probably to help heal me by sharing the memories and the revenge. Three other people to share the burden had to be better than one or two, didn't it? And I was grateful for that. It was kind of even working. But still, there was a certain homicidal zip missing from the thing.

"Again," Blaire said.

"Murder's no answer," Tina said.

We all looked at her. It wasn't cool to preach to somebody else even when you're supposedly saving them from the electric chair.

"It is for me," I said. "As far as I can tell. And it also keeps you guys out of trouble."

"I'd miss you too much," Blaire said, meaning after I was "sent up."

Blaire. The fact that she'd pretty much taken over the direction of my life since she'd arrived was a surprisingly pleasant experience, particularly when I didn't try to fight it. Besides, the truth was while I still wanted to see my mother die I didn't want to pay for it now that I had somebody good to live for.

"There's no way I can get away with it?" I asked them one last time.

"No way," Doris said.

"It isn't that we'd tell you did it," Tina said.

"You sent the cops a map ten years ago," Blaire said.

"Okay," I said before they knew what hit them, "then I've got an idea."

My *poem*

Unconditional Love

We are twins, you and I
Joined at the waist
By one super set of
internal organs.
From birth
To death
We stare at each other
Our four eyes one
Unless we are reading
In which case we look
Over each other's
right shoulder at the book
We're holding there.
Or unless we are sleeping
In which case we close
our eyes and dream
identical dreams about
the surgical separation
We both know won't
ever take place
because of all
the bloody snakes
we share.

Of course they had to do it my way. When the resistant one comes up with her own plan you're practically honor bound to go for it. Plus, after all, the intended victim was my mother.

"Did you see how all three of your plans reflected some hidden fear you've got, some shadowy, albeit symbolic, psychosexual nightmare you might not even be aware of?" I said. I paused while they shifted.

"Being Smothered, Being Noticed, Being Ignored," I said. I smiled smugly and then I drank an entire glass of water while they figured out which went with which.

"What we're missing is what's my mother's big thing."

"But we don't know her," Tina said.

"Blaire's idea was the closest," I said. "We have to humiliate my mother in front of a bunch of people she admires. And I know the perfect place to do it. But the big thing we have to do is make her apologize."

"And that won't be easy," Blaire said. "Some people are constitutionally incapable of it."

"And she has to mean it," I said, which was the wild card I was keeping up my sleeve. My mother might apologize to get us off her neck but she'd always be keeping her fingers crossed behind her back, figuratively speaking. She'd always have to have the last word.

The next thing we had to do was scripts; we had to do costumes; we had to do our hair and makeup. We had to draw maps to scale. We even had to block out our moves in the school gym on a couple of weekends when the teams weren't home. But first, before any of this, we had to do something none of us really wanted to do at all.

We had to put Doris on the wagon and we had to make her stay there.

Why?

Because she did three bad things in one week and we didn't have a choice.

She blacked out. She forgot the contents of one entire evening's worth of planning when it was all about her role as Mother Superior. The next morning she didn't remember one thing we'd discussed.

She sprained her wrist. She came to work with the thing all bandaged up and told us she'd slipped getting out of the bathtub the night before. Which was probably the truth.

She embarrassed us at a restaurant by chewing out the server in such a rabid manner that it took our breath away. The server had merely, by mistake, substituted an onion for an olive in her dry martini.

I realized I loved her so much it hurt.

But enough was enough. We had to have yet another meeting, this time when Doris was busy with the Board of Trustees. Then we had to buy a book about making interventions, and then we had to do one.

When I say "we" I mean me and Blaire and Tina. They helped me with this too even though I was really the friend. The book said that interventions are better the more people you pull in to confront the drinker.

It didn't work at all.

"Thank you very much," Doris said to us, flat. I was weeping; Tina was twitching and Blaire was playing with her nails. We were in Doris's green and white kitchen, on her turf, which wasn't advised by the experts, but it was Saturday morning and she wouldn't move.

"It must have taken a great deal of courage to come to me with this," she said.

"Would you like to talk about it?" I said, from the textbook, verbatim.

"No," Doris said and that was the end of that.

Until the car accident.

Perhaps accident is too strong a word for what actually happened. Doris ran her car over a purebred German shepherd stud in the prime of life and then had to sit with his distraught owner until the police and the animal rescue team arrived. She felt terrible about what she'd done although the dog had been chasing a ball into the middle of the street when she hit it and had died instantly. But, besides all that, the police officer taking the report noticed the distinct smell of Scotch on her breath. At eleven o'clock in the morning.

She was released into our custody after the officer found out that she was the principal of a Catholic high school and had once upon a time, been a nun. His brother had been a priest.

"She's been going through some hard times lately, Officer," Blaire said.

"We'll make sure to get her to AA," I said. "She's had her very last drink." With this, I looked Doris straight in the eye and extracted a pound of flesh. She nodded at me and I took her hand to seal this bond.

33

We spared Tina the direct and difficult second experience with Doris, but we told her about it later. Meanwhile she had plenty of time to fall in love and be a real lesbian again.

She looked as rosy and shining as she could be. She looked like a delicious apple or a strawberry pie. I was almost envious except that I was still pretty excited about Blaire. What did gall me was that she got to be a lesbian and have a nice mother too.

"Oh, you two," Tina said. "Pammy's right outside, waiting for me." Tina had stopped by on a Saturday morning to give us the news before breakfast.

"Well, ask her to come in then," Blaire said, like the amiable old dad.

"You do fall in love rather often," I said, but only because I thought I should.

Actually I thought it was so charming to fall in love and then have to tell everybody, arms open wide like all the world belonged to you.

"You're the only ones I could tell," Tina said.

Except that it wasn't quite as fun if you were a lesbian because you had to pick and choose.

But anybody would have fallen in love with Pammy. She was dark and deep but innocent still. She looked you right in the eye when you spoke or when she was speaking to you and she told me and Blaire right off how much she'd wanted to meet us. And she meant it, I swear she did.

"So how long have you been a lesbian, Pammy?" I said.

"Since junior high," she said. "Since kindergarten."

"What?" I gasped. Tina laughed at me. I was such a stale vegetable right now.

"I always loved girls and women," Pammy said. "I kept thinking I would grow out of it. I kept thinking it was just because I wanted a better mother. But, oh well . . ." She took Tina's hand gently, tentatively, not like she owned her already. Pammy was perfect.

How did some people get so honest? She wasn't afraid of saying anything, was she?

"You're mystifying her a little bit," Blaire said, after Pammy and Tina left to go to brunch. "She's only nineteen years old, for God's sake."

"You don't change much after nineteen," I said. We were watching women's tennis on TV where all the girls were nineteen too. Everybody was suddenly nineteen. "I didn't."

"You're wrong," Blaire said. "Look how much you've changed since we met." I suppose she meant I was more open and loving, more trusting about telling what had happened to me. But in some ways I was exactly the same. I still wished my mother would be dead.

34

But she wasn't. Not at all. She wouldn't give up. She kept writing me letters all this time and calling my tape. She, who hadn't called me in ten years was suddenly desperate to be my best friend.

"Hello, darling," she'd chirp. "It's Mommie dearest. You certainly are the busy type. Could you find it in your heart to call me back? I miss you. I love you."

"Hi Sweetie," she wrote in big, loopy script inside a card with a drawing of the cutest little girl on the cover, swinging, skirts flying.

Greeting Card Poem

> You're the nicest daughter anyone could be
> The best of all is that you're part of me
> Gentle and loving and pretty too
> The second best thing is I'm part of you.

Love, Mommie dearest

P.S. Let's all get together again soon. Bring some of your poems. Blaire said you're writing too.

I wasn't. I'd only written that one poem since Blaire got here. There didn't seem to be much point to it now that I had a live-in poet to do it for me. The trouble was, I didn't think Blaire was writing any poems either. All my problems were taking up too much space.

My mother also sent me a cotton sweater and a pair of socks. She sent us a signed black-and-white studio portrait in a silver frame from which she gazed at us longingly. She sent us tickets to Peter, Paul and Mary in concert. I made Blaire sell them at the gate. I was sure my mother had bought the seats right next to ours.

"I love Peter, Paul and Mary," Blaire said when the tickets first arrived. She sang, " 'The answer my friend is blowing in the wind,' " and then she stuck out her lower lip. "You're being sort of psycho."

"Then trade them for other seats," I said.

"They're sold out," Blaire said.

"She did this on purpose to cause friction and disharmony," I said. "She's right here in the room with us, leering."

The good thing was that Blaire never tried to get me to take pity on my mother. Not like I'd done to Tina when she was mad at hers. But I hardly ever let Blaire out of my sight just in case she took pity on my mother herself.

"Don't leave me," I said, late one evening. I held both Blaire's hands in my own and cried a little bit to show her I really meant it.

"I have to have some peanut M&M's," Blaire said. "I crave them. Immediately. You can come with me and sit in the car. You don't even have to change from your nightgown."

But I couldn't go. I'd told Doris I'd be by the phone all night in case she wanted a drink while her sponsor was out of town.

"Oh, go then," I said. I was trying to think about how, after Blaire left, I could make a chive and cheese omelette and eat it all by myself or I could smoke a cigarette without Blaire waving at the air in front of her and telling me to go outside. I could masturbate in the living room with Miss December folded out on the coffee table, begging to watch.

Instead I sat in the dark bathroom on the tile counter and stared out the window at the street, counting headlights until

Blaire got home. And it wasn't until she came in the front door, laughing and unwrapping me a Hostess Twinkie Light, that I realized that this was now, not then. It wasn't when I was six or seven or eight and I used to wait for my mother to come home in her white T-Bird, drunk and sexy and angry at me for still being wide awake.

And then I had to remember a whole set of other things she'd done to me when she found me in the bathroom sitting by the window, half asleep and still waiting.

"I can't handle being the one with all the problems," I said, in the dark, in the bathroom. We were sitting fully clothed in the empty bathtub facing each other, touching toes. We'd put a candle on the counter in front of the mirror.

"It's pretty in here like this," Blaire said. She was so happy with her M&M's. She kept popping them into her mouth, one by one, and smiling as she chewed. "Right now you're reclaiming the bathroom from your mother when she used to touch you in there. And you're reclaiming the bedroom with me."

"I'm sick of being the sick one," I said.

"The identified sick one," she said sweetly. "It's my turn when you're done."

That made me feel better but I knew it wasn't true. In any pair, who doesn't like being the one on top?

35

"Oh, what the hell," Doris said, three weeks later on the unseasonably hot deck of our rented Christmas cabin in the woods. I had just told her she ought to put on some clothes, even if only a T-shirt or bathrobe because we might want to rent the place again.

"No one can see me," she said. "It's all pine branches up here. Perfectly lovely view. And I'm part of it. Part of the trees. A clean and sober goddess of the forest."

"A regular Diana," Blaire said. She thought Doris was pretty funny now that she was so busy doing everything for the first time in years.

It wasn't that Doris's body was bad to look at anymore. She'd dropped lots of alcohol bloat and you could see exactly where the muscles were going to be after a few weeks with the personal fitness trainer she'd hired.

"Look," Doris said to me, "if it makes you uncomfortable I'll put some clothes on. But I at least want you to know what's going on in my mind about it."

Doris was big on telling us what was in her mind since she'd stopped drinking. Doris was a lot more boring now than she had been before but they tell you that's going to happen at first. She was boring now except for the uncomfortable incidents she kept pulling.

"I have to do these stunts every so often to help me not miss drinking," she said. "I'm convincing myself that life is more surprising and enjoyable without it."

Doris had gotten a tattoo with Blaire three days before at a place near the Navy yard. It was a tiny red skull and crossbones to represent death and rebirth.

Now, looking at it on her naked hip, I told her she should have gotten a phoenix or a scorpion, something more positive, but she said she wanted dark, dark, dark. I told her she was a dry drunk the way she needed to jack herself up with thrills. Tina, who had just been listening until now, told me I was way off, that Doris, without alcohol, was more free and expansive and alive than she had been before, when she used to drink and live through me.

"You miss that, huh?" Blaire said, in front of everybody. "Her needing you that way." It was true. I missed the way Doris used to spend so much of her energy on me before she got healthy and started to care about herself. I missed it so much I almost didn't like her anymore.

"No," I yelled. For some reason I'd started shouting at everybody.

"What is with you?" Blaire shouted back.

"I don't know," I said but I did. It was the mother caper. For me, the idea of it wasn't working that much anymore.

"I read that if people are deviant in one way they often try to make up for it by trying to be as conservative as possible everyplace else," Tina said.

Tina was reading whatever she could get her hands on about the homosexual experience ever since she'd decided for sure she was one. And the truth was I didn't much like her either now that she had a full-time girlfriend of her own. Nobody needed me anymore except Blaire and that didn't seem to be nearly enough.

"I'm going to be careful of that. Tell me if you notice me slipping into that, would you?" Tina said.

Besides hiring a personal fitness trainer, Doris had gone to an astrologer, bought a dog, restyled her hair (with Tina's help), taken up Qi Qong, met a nice man and put her house on the market. All in the few weeks since she'd stopped drinking.

"I've created a monster," I said. Nobody heard me.

Maybe I was talking about me. While Doris was getting perfect not only had I stopped making love; I was getting fat, teaching unprepared and generally hating the world.

"So when are we going to do the mom thing?" Doris said, stepping into her underpants, finally.

"I told you," I said. "A week after the Showcase House opens. We have to case it out. We have to do a silent dress rehearsal. We have to make sure about her schedule."

We'd come to the mountains to plan and practice. We'd also come because we deserved it. We'd been through a lot.

"I want to do it now," Doris said. She obviously hadn't studied the part in AA about staying sober through embracing delayed gratification.

"Don't be stupid," I said. "My mother isn't even here. Besides we need the Showcase House atmosphere for setting and audience. This is performance art, Doris. This is psychosexual guerrilla theater. And I want it perfect so we don't have to do it again." I was trying to be earnest and convincing, as if, after the event, I would be all healed. I was still trying to believe it myself.

Tina and Blaire went inside. Doris got up and sniffed. "I'm going to my room to write a poem," she said, like now that she was sober, she could do it all.

If they wouldn't let me murder my mother, this pretend part had to be great.

PRODUCTION NOTES

Costumes	*Props*
Doris—habit	rosary, riding whip
me—nightgown	dolly, nursing bottle
Blaire—formal gown	megaphone, pom-poms
Tina—school uniform	magic wand, weight scales

SETTING

Twentieth Annual Junior Philharmonic Showcase House of Design. The sponsors take a huge estate, use the donated services of decorators and suppliers to renovate and redecorate and then charge fifteen bucks a head for people to walk through the thing. The profits then get sent to the symphony. (It was my mother's favorite volunteer activity for obvious reasons. She wasn't exactly the type to waitress at a soup kitchen, if you know what I mean.)

Blaire had given us all lines to recite in the rooms my mother was assigned to cover. As I recalled from the times I'd gone with her, each volunteer had several locations where she was supposed to watch for pilfering and answer questions or offer information on the history of the house or the intentions of the decorator. My mother was very good at all of the above. She was good at handling several things at once.

And we were going to be very good at public humiliation. In front of all her rich friends sometimes we would speak in unison, a Greek chorus of harpies. Sometimes we would speak antiphonally, overlapping with powerful inevitability as we layered out our rage. Sometimes we would each have an archetypal role that required dialogue or a speech. The script was damned good too. We were seriously considering publication after the show was over. Not many people get a Pulitzer prize winner to write the book for the grand opera of their revenge.

After awhile, I roused myself and called everybody back out on the deck.

"Okay," I said. "Let's practice."

"Good," Doris said. "We haven't practiced since I stopped drinking. I wonder if my acting's improved."

"Why now?" Blaire said.

"Why not now?" I said. "Don't you want to do it anymore?" I watched her try to answer. "You look shifty."

"I just don't think we should overpractice," she said. "People in theater always say you should avoid that so you'll peak during the performance."

"Oh," I said.

"Come on, Blaire," Tina said. "Let's do a rehearsal and then you look over my sestinas and villanelles." Blaire was putting Tina through lots of rigid verse forms as poetic initiation rites or something.

"Okay," she said.

"You be the mother," I said.

"No," Blaire said. "You be her. So you know how it feels."

"Why?" I said.

"So you can better direct us," Doris said. "That's a good point."

I wasn't sure if that was what Blaire was after but I agreed anyway. "And I'll be me too?" I said.

"Sure," Tina said. "It's your trip. We're only along for the ride."

"All right," I said. "Let's do the kitchen scene. Doris, you need your habit, Tina, the nightgown and Blaire, the formal. Bring down the whip, nursing bottle, pom-poms and magic wand."

KITCHEN SCENE

MOTHER: (To Showcase visitors clustered in the triangle between the butcher board preparation island, Sub-Zero refrigerator and Wolf range) This is the center of the house, the kitchen created by James Owens and Julia Ferraro of Owens-Ferraro Bath and Kitchen. Primary consideration was given to providing adequate counter space for a couple who entertains extensively without sacrificing convenience. Lots of light from these halogen tracts, country charm from the tasteful use of painted country tile and whitewashed pine.

ME: (In school uniform, huge rosary around neck) I'm home. Where's the just-baked ginger cookies? Where's the milk?

MOTHER: Excuse me? This isn't your home. This is the Junior Philharmonic Showcase House of Design. You must be confused, dear. Who did you say you were?

ME: I'm your daughter and goddammit, I'm hungry. I'm always hungry. This fabulous kitchen and you never lift a pot.

MOTHER: Good God. You are my daughter. But you're far too old to be wearing a school uniform. (Lifts the rosary) And we weren't Catholics. We were Episcopalians.

DORIS: (Entering) That's my cue, isn't it?

ME: No.

DORIS: (Exiting) It should be. This script needs some action.

BLAIRE: (Entering in evening gown with magic wand) It's my cue. See if this refreshes your memory, Mom. Come here, baby. (Waves wand) I'll give you some cookies. I'll give you some cookies and a beautiful home if you'll lie down on this butcher block preparation island and lift up the skirt of your school uniform so I can examine your pretty rosebud labia.

MOTHER: What the hell are you doing? You can't do that here. Is that Blaire Bennett? You can't do that here. You must be crazy. Ladies and gentlemen, these people are communist demonstrators illegally protesting the Junior Philharmonic way of life. Pay them no mind. Move right on to the Country French Laundry Room. (No one moves)

TINA: (Enters, carrying pom-poms and wearing nightgown. Watches as Blaire pretends to push her wand in and out of my vagina) Push it in, push it in, way in.

MOTHER: Stop it. This is disgusting. Don't do that in the kitchen.

ME: (Lifts up head) Shall we move to the Little Girl's Bedroom perhaps? You did it there too.

MOTHER: (To audience) Avert your eyes. (To me) All right, you be a good girl and stop this disgusting display and I'll bake you cookies. Jump down now. I need the preparation area for rolling the dough.

TINA: It'll take more than cookies, lady. Give me an A, give me an A, give me a P, give me a P, give me an O, give me an O, give me an L, give me an L. (Stops) This part kind of drags, don't you think? Maybe we could just make a banner with the word APOLOGY printed on it.

DORIS: (Enters) My turn?

ME: Okay. Don't forget the whip.

DORIS: I've got the whip.

MOTHER: Who the hell are you? I'm not even Catholic.

DORIS: Ask forgiveness, Mom, or we'll do this for hours all over the house. (Snaps whip) We'll tell all these generous ticket holders about how you put your perfectly manicured fingers up your little girl's vagina and used her proximity to bring yourself to orgasm. (Snaps whip again) We'll tell all these aesthetically sensitive visitors how a chronic child molester can move amongst them, leaning against expensive Corian counters, living a lie without ever being exposed as the sick pervert that she truly is. Until now. Bend over that kitchen stool and take your thirty lashes, Mom, and we won't press charges. Apologize to your daughter in front of all these people and we'll make sure none of this gets into the paper at all. (Pause) What if she won't bend over?

BLAIRE: She will.

I applauded my actors' energy but now I didn't even want to do it anymore. For one thing, I knew my mother would never apologize, even if somebody held a gun to her head. For another, even if the torture worked and she was reduced to a sniveling centipede, she'd still be inside me, eating away. She'd still be alive.

"So how did you feel as the Mother?" Blaire said.

"Annoyed," I said. "Somewhat."

"You weren't humiliated?" Tina asked. "It wasn't the worst moment of your life?"

"No," I said. "I think we looked more ridiculous than she did."

"That was a good line she got off about the Marxists," Doris said.

"Communists," I said.

"You didn't feel her suffering?" Blaire said.

"What suffering?" I said. "I'm the one who's suffering. I'm the victim here. Did you forget that, Blaire? Is it more comfortable for you to identify with the perpetrator?"

"Blaire didn't say that," Tina said. "She wants you to get some satisfactory catharsis. Why do you think she's stayed here so long? For you, to help you with all of this."

"Stop telling me what Blaire's trying to say," I shouted. "I know what she's trying to say. She's trying to say I deserved what I got."

Even I knew that Blaire wasn't saying that but I was getting a little worried about the steadiness of her allegiance to the cause. She was sounding awfully sympathetic to Mom.

"Let's leave her alone for a while," Doris said, meaning me. "No one else can fix it for her."

Everybody left to entertain themselves and I stayed out on the deck again. I didn't mind being left alone all the time but I wished, at least, somebody had told me what "it" was.

I took off my T-shirt, shorts and underpants and folded them neatly by the Adirondack chair. I sat down like Doris had, naked, and closed my eyes. Maybe she knew something I didn't about living life right. Like undressing yourself on a public deck in mid-morning was saying the hell with everybody else. And if I could do that, wouldn't murder be beside the point?

36

After a while Blaire came back outside and said, "Come to our room, my love."

"But it's only ten in the morning," I said. I was whining. I was such a drag. Now that I was naked, I wanted to go all the way. I wanted to climb out of my own skin.

"You have to trust me better," Blaire said a little later, naked next to me, under our blue and white comforter.

"I want to be happy, Blaire, I really do, but there's always something wrong," I said. "I mean, here we are, floating together under this soft and downy cloud and I am so sad. I want to start over."

"You can't," she said.

"If I'd started out right, I'd be such a better person," I said. I began to pull on her nipple with my mouth.

"Ouch," Blaire said. "Don't forget you have teeth now."

"See?" I said. "I lied. This relationship is based on lies. I do have a mother thing for you. I want you to nurse me into a happy adulthood."

Blaire ran her fingers through my hair.

"I have nothing to offer you," I said. "I am a sterile, self-pitying narcissist, sucking the lifeblood from everybody around me. And, I didn't really want Doris to get well."

"I love you," Blaire said. "I'll do it."

"What?" I said.

"I'll nurse you into a happy adulthood," she said. "If I can."

"You haven't written one goddamn poem since you came to stay with me, have you?" I said.

"I've been keeping a journal," Blaire said, "with snippets of this and that."

"If I were good for you you'd be filling page upon page with lines of craft and truth," I said. "Pulitzer material, not flaccid vacation stuff."

"We've only been together a month," she said. She pulled the covers up over both our heads as if that would help. "I'm not worried."

"Can't you see that I'm smothering you?" I said.

"It isn't going to work, dearie," she whispered, putting her fingers on my lips.

"Shit," I said. "Can't you see that you're smothering me?"

And then she kissed me all over my body, as if one place was just as good as another.

"Blaire," I said after a few minutes.

"Oh no," she said because I'd been having so much trouble lately, since remembering about my mother. For weeks, if we did it at all, I had to practically fax Blaire a blueprint of what I wanted beforehand.

"Okay," I'd say, "but don't go inside me and don't touch my clitoris directly. Stay above it and to one side.

"An inch to the left," I'd say in the middle. "Faster, please and harder and bring up some wetness but remember you aren't supposed to go inside."

God. It was miserable but I guess it was better than nothing. This time I only wanted to ask her a question.

"You never told me any of your secrets," I said. Blaire's secrets had to be at least as good as mine: "I tried to murder my mom." She even had a tattoo on her leg about it.

"Now?" she said. "You have to hear a secret now?"

"Yeah," I said. "The big one."

"I haven't ranked them, exactly," Blaire said. Which meant, of course, that she had.

"A good one," I said. "You know what I mean."

"Why?" she said.

"I've told you mine, for one thing," I said. "For another, you want me to trust you more. If you do this, I'll know you better; I'll trust you more."

"It's a test," she said.

She was right. It was her final exam. If she passed this, she'd be mine forever.

"Okay," I said. "It's a test."

"I've always wanted to be a man," Blaire said.

"The male role, power, freedom, respect?" I said.

"No," she said. "Physically. I wanted a hairy chest and a penis."

"No," I said. "Stop kidding around." But she wasn't smiling. In fact she was breathing so rapidly and shallowly that I was worried she might faint. This was a big secret, for sure.

"It's true," she said. "Don't make this hard on me. I never got a sex change because I think that's stupid. I like my body fine. I just always would rather be a man."

I looked at her for a long time.

In some ways, I wished she was. Most men were so easy to comprehend it wasn't funny. Of course, if she'd been a man I wouldn't have loved her in the first place.

"I didn't say I wanted to be with a man," Blaire said. "I didn't say I like men. It's too hard to explain."

"Would you like to be a man with me?" I said. People's sexual stuff usually didn't faze me at all. It was mostly so cut off or so primitively based that it had a whole separate life of its own. If Blaire's deepest fantasy was to get on top of me with a dildo strapped around her waist, and pump like mad, well, what the hell?

"I don't know," she said.

"It's okay with me," I said.

"I never told it to anybody before," Blaire said.

Finally. I was finally full. I took her hand in mine. That was the thing I wanted to hear, that it was a virgin secret, mined just for me. The content of the secret was practically irrelevant.

"Whatever you want to do with me is fine," I said. I wasn't

just being open-minded and good-hearted, like a well-paid whore. The idea of Blaire wanting to be a man was beginning to sort of turn me on. It was beginning to feel better than being a baby.

37

Later somebody was knocking at our bedroom door. I was busy having a full-out dream even though it was only noon. It was a nightmare about a flat tire in the middle of a red-hot desert.

So I was glad somebody was knocking, until they said why.

Tina came in and sat down on the edge of the bed.

"Your mother's here," she said. "She's brought lunch for all of us. It looks great. Cold lobster, artichokes, wine and French bread. Shall I take the food and send her away?"

"Blaire?" I said.

"I'll go talk to her," she said, putting on her jeans. "How did she find us?"

"She found us because you told her where we were," I said to her. Suddenly I knew why she had been pulling on my empathy so much, like it was a long gooey piece of saltwater taffy.

"She said she followed us all the way from the city," Tina said. "I asked her the same thing. She was very matter-of-fact about it."

"Did she disarm you?" I said to her after Blaire left.

"Not at all," Tina said. "You do look like her, though."

"Go get me a sharp kitchen knife like a good girl, would you?" I said. "I have to slice an apple."

"What?" Tina said.

"Only kidding," I said, "about the apple."

I listened to their voices downstairs while I put on my clothes; my mother's smooth, eager inflection and Blaire's deep, firm tones blended into a kind of composition that made me dizzy with killer rage.

I went to the top of the stairs and looked down at the two of them putting the food out on the table. Doris and Tina were out on the deck playing Scrabble. They'd been keeping a running score for more than a week, moving the game to wherever we were going next.

"I do like your hair," my mother was saying to Blaire. Then she actually ran her palm over Blaire's spiky white crown.

Blaire didn't step away from her or say "don't do that."

I gripped the banister tight. My skin began to burn up on my bones. My legs were shaking. I was on the edge of everything.

"Thanks," Blaire said. "I don't mean to be rude but your daughter doesn't exactly want to see you."

"I came to see you," my mother said, "actually."

I swallowed and loosened my grip. They still looked good together, Blaire and my mother.

"You look different," Blaire was saying. "You have your face lifted since the last time?"

"I reread all your work," my mother said.

"Thanks," Blaire said again. "I need to talk to you about what you did to her when she was growing up."

"Who?" my mother said.

"Your daughter," Blaire said.

"I wasn't perfect," my mother said. "But who is? Are you?"

By the time I screamed "Fuck you both" loud as hell from the top of the stairs Blaire and my mother had already left the cabin to go for a walk in the woods.

"I don't think anything's going to work, really," I said to Doris later. She was busy disemboweling her very own lobster. "Killing her, confronting her. I'm always going to be a mess." I was sure about that. What I wasn't sure about was what Blaire was up to. What was she doing handling my mother for me? I couldn't decide whether to be angry or relieved.

"One day at a time," Doris said, absently cracking a claw.

"Once somebody has ruined your childhood, there's no way to get it back," I said.

"Powerless," Doris said. She wasn't listening at all.

"Once your worldview is set, it's set," I said.

"Never get too tired or too hungry," Doris said, dipping an artichoke leaf in mayonnaise and then dragging it under her front teeth.

"Once a parent treats you like shit, you feel like shit the rest of your life," I said. "No matter what. It's simple imprinting."

"Try God," Doris said, handing me a buttery piece of the French bread.

"Stop with the AA slogans," I said, taking the bread. "Are you listening at all?"

"No," she said. "I'm eating. One thing at a time."

So while she ate I opened the bottle of white wine my mother had brought to go with the lobster and drank the whole thing down. Tina and Doris just watched me.

I kept asking myself questions like: why did my mother always have to take what I had? And, who did she really hate and why was I always the stand-in? The questions didn't seem to have answers. They just repeated themselves, over and over.

"The sky is spinning," I slurred after a few minutes.

Revenge was what I had to have. Revenge was the gift I would give to myself. My mother never gave me anything. Now she could give me her pain.

"You're drunk," Tina said. "On one bottle of wine."

It was three o'clock and my mother and Blaire still weren't back. I was lying faceup on the deck, trying not to picture them doing it on a bed of pine needles. I'd thought the wine would help. It hadn't. All it did was make everything seem more possible. Betrayal, murder, hell.

"I guess one of us has to be the drinker," Doris said, staring down at me from the branch of a pine tree. "Some families are constituted like that."

"At least in this condition she can't kill her," Tina said like I wasn't there.

"I'm still here," I said and then I turned over on my side and threw up.

"Ick," Tina said.

"Get the hose," said Doris, "and spray her down. It's nice she did it on the deck at least."

And this wasn't even my lowest point.

38

When I woke up it was almost dark out. I was still on the deck, in the same position I'd passed out in and I was a little damp from being hosed off. Still, I felt pretty good considering all I'd put myself through. Until I remembered why I'd gotten drunk in the first place.

"Blaire," I shouted. I shouldn't have had to. Any decent lover who'd just been in the dim and teeming woods with my mother, the forest wolf, should have been outside in the almost dark with me, cradling my head with velvety guilt and concern. I waited for a long time. The lights were on in the house but evidently nobody was around to answer me.

"Tina," I shouted. So what that I wasn't at my best, again? I wasn't Tina's teacher anymore. Even though I was barely acting like an adult, I was now her peer, her friend. So what that she had to see me take off my clothes and be sick to my stomach both in the same day? Weren't there all these side benefits like my drama with my mother and my teaching her about being a lesbian and life in general? And that through me she'd gotten to know famous gifted Blaire and her own ex-high school principal as a person?

"Doris," I shouted. This time my voice cracked pathetically. I was getting a little bit scared. I felt like I was in a bloody fairy tale that hadn't been written for kids at all. I didn't want to get up and find out that there wasn't anybody in the house when I was out here in the middle of nowhere with my mother, the rabid wolf, out prowling the woods.

"Mother," I whispered. I turned over and looked around. She was there, behind me, smoking a cigarette, in the shadows. While I was asleep, she could have kicked me in the face or slit my throat or put something wicked in my mouth to make me gag.

"We need to have a talk," she said.

"No, we don't," I said.

"Your friends seem to think so," she said. "They drove into town so we could be alone."

I stood up so I would be taller than her. I leaned over her so she would stop talking to me and go home.

"You are far too old to be hating me like this," she said. "It's very unattractive."

"How do you know I hate you?" I said.

"Blaire confirmed it," she said. "But it's quite obvious. We both agreed you simply need to grow up and get on with your life."

"You conned her," I said. "You got my friends to leave me. You got them to trust your intentions."

"You need to let go of your obsession," my mother said.

"You need to apologize for what you did to me," I said. "And then you need to do about a hundred other things and then just maybe I'll consider it."

She was right, of course, and that's what made this whole conversation so annoying. I was giving my life away for nothing. But, still, it wasn't her place to tell me that. It was her place to grovel at my feet and lick them clean.

"Blaire is too old for you," she said. "You're obviously acting out your unresolved feelings for me."

"You're the one who climbed into my bed," I said.

"Blaire kissed me," my mother said, "on our walk. That's why we were gone so long. She said I tasted like a woman."

I could see that she was smiling and holding her cigarette away from her body like a movie star. I took it out of her fingers and put it out. I knew Blaire wouldn't say something as stupid as that she tasted like a woman which meant my mother was lying. But it didn't matter what lies my mother said. I wasn't sure how but I did know that I was going to kill her. And this time I wasn't going to fuck it up.

Lest you object that matricide is ugly, childish and an inappropriate subject to investigate in a love story like this one—lest you believe that because I'm an adult lover of women I should know better, think about all the great female mother haters who wished they'd had my guts. Think about Christina Crawford. Think about all the mother haters who pretended instead to worship the ground their mothers walked on and put their real feelings inside causing the decay of stomach lining and mental health. Think of Sylvia Plath.

What got me through the next hour of this unplanned visit with my mother was not thinking about the mother haters but thinking about how I was going to do what they couldn't.

While she unloaded on me all her unhappy excuses of childhood abuse, miserable adolescence and misunderstood adulthood, I painted grotesque pictures in my head. While my mother described her own father's insatiable delight in young female flesh, including her own, I put a hemp noose around her neck and kicked out the chair.

While, once again, she offered up the names and proclivities of all the lovers she'd ever had, boys and girls, mostly wealthy and white and married to each other, I poured acid on her face and watched it eat away her nasal passages and dental work.

While she explained that she loved me more than life and so what if she'd been a little bit neglectful, I put a pillow over her head and held it there, riding her resistant muscle spasms like she was a horse.

"I should have gotten you a dog," my mother said. Now she looked at me, to see, I think, if she'd made me squirm.

"Would you like a drink?" I said.

"Or had another child. I tried, God knows I tried," she said, "but your father must have had a low sperm count."

"Gin?" I said.

"You aren't going to lace it with anything?" She laughed. "He didn't really enjoy sex, I don't think," she said. "He had a tiny, tiny penis."

My mother was indeed a beautiful woman. I watched her light another cigarette and blow out the match. What a waste, it seemed to me. All her beauty did was make it easier for her to hurt other people and squander her life.

"Bring me that drink now, would you?" she said. And then, "I was never angry at my parents. I adored them, lock, stock and barrel. Like you should."

I did look a lot like her, I couldn't help but notice in the mirror on my way to get her the drink. Except that my features weren't so even or so fine. Maybe, like a gigantic bad joke, I was getting to look more and more like her the older I got.

"How do you know those other ones?" she said after I handed her the gin.

"Doris and Tina, my friends from where I work," I said. "They wanted to come to the cabin for the holidays."

"There's no television," my mother said. We were still on the deck, in the dark. It seemed easier to be with her outside where we were mere flyspecks under the enormous ceiling of sky. And where I didn't have to look at her face or show her mine at all.

"No television," I said.

"I like television," my mother said. She had been quite smart once but now who could tell what was happening inside her head. Word processing, maybe, and wishful thinking. "But I did come here to talk to you."

"No, you didn't," I said. "You came to steal Blaire from me."

"I'm sure Blaire has a mind of her own," my mother said.

"Please go home," I said.

"If I was home now I'd be watching *Murder She Wrote* with Angela Lansbury," she said, wistfully. "I hope they never take that off the air no matter how old she gets. They can just prop her up in a wheelchair and keep giving her face-lifts."

"Maybe you'll go first, before Angela does," I said.

"Go? You mean die?" she said. "Then say die. I hate euphemisms for the word 'death.' "

"Die," I said. "Die, die, die."

"You'd like that," she said. I couldn't really see her expression anymore at all. But I didn't need to. I'd made a discovery. She wanted me to hate her. She liked it. And she wanted me to kill her, to try to kill her again, too. She wanted me to feel bad. The worse I felt, the better it was for her.

But why?

"Why aren't they back yet?" I asked her. Why had Blaire set this up and then left me, defenseless, with the person I hated most in the world?

"I don't know," she said. "Maybe they went to the movies. It's starting to rain. Didn't you feel that drop? I may have to spend the night."

Then she stood up.

She'd planned all this, of course. Right down to the rain. If not that, it would have been a flat tire.

I followed her into the house and sat down across from her at the dining room table where all the food had been laid out earlier. The table was cleared off now and there was a glass jar filled with things from the woods: a small pine bough, a couple of yellow leaves, a branch of berries.

"Blaire and I picked these," my mother said. She lit a cigarette. "The gin," she said waving her glass for a refill. I went into the kitchen to find the bottle I'd brought. It was cheap gin and she'd probably notice but I didn't care. Or I wouldn't care after I finished her off, did her in, ended the matter. Killed her.

"Let's talk about your lesbianism," my mother said after I poured some more gin into her glass. She made it sound like a disease: your hypothyroidism, your rheumatism, your giantism. "As you know, I myself am quite vigorously heterosexual. A few women have caught my fancy over the years but not because they were women. Rather, in spite of it."

I wondered how Blaire, Tina and Doris would feel about finding a dead body in the cabin and if they'd help me dig a hole deep enough to keep her under for good.

"Blaire, of course, is one of those," my mother was saying. "She's really more like a man than a woman, isn't she?" I wondered if Blaire had told my mother her big secret too.

"Remember the time I needed money for school texts," I said, "and you had your lawyer write me a letter to put me off."

"No," my mother said.

"That made me want to kill you," I said. "I went to sleep every night in my dorm room and dreamed about chopping your head off with an ax."

She looked up at me. I thought I noticed a slight frisson, a thrilled intake of breath.

"You should have gotten a job," she said.

"It was only fifty dollars," I said. "I already had two jobs."

"I must have been worried about your continuing dependency," she said.

"I'd been on my own for five years," I said.

"Maybe there was a recession," she said. "I can't recall now. Why do you so need to live in the past?"

"I can't seem to selectively forget the hard parts," I said. "Like when I found you in bed with Leo Martin and he called me a nosy little shithead and you just pulled the covers over your head?"

"You embarrassed me," she said.

"I was five years old," I said. I was thinking about all the times she'd made fun of me in front of my friends, like she and I were in competition. And how she always won.

"What a long memory you have," she said. "One has to go on." She was smiling. She was right. She was taunting me. I think she wanted me to tell her about more of my murder fantasies. Maybe she was pretending to be Angela herself, getting me all worked up to try something just before the rumpled cop leaped into the hotel room. Balance and goodness restored.

Of course, this wasn't at all like that. My mother, the potential victim, was bad; I, the potential murderer, was a good person pushed to the limit. No court on earth would convict me. I was like a battered wife, ribs broken, eyes blackened once too often.

Well, they did still sometimes convict battered women who murdered but it was an unpopular verdict, the kind *MS* magazine and NOW spoke out against until it was overturned in a higher court. Phew. And then, if you were just a little lucky, you, the murderer, would get a Movie-of-the-Week offer or at least a ghost-written autobiography for sale near the cash register at the supermarket.

I looked at my mother almost fondly. She was sipping her drink. She thought I was angry with her but she was wrong. I was going to be famous and revered because of her. They'd invent a new syndrome based on my experience as a Battered Adult Daughter—BAD. I'd be on all the talk shows, on the cover of all the gossip magazines. I'd be more famous than Blaire for a while anyway. People like me flash out pretty fast, but no matter. I'd write a book called *The Dead Mother* and invest the profits, live comfortably, if not luxuriously, for the rest of my life. And with no mother, on top of it all.

"I'd like you to run me a bath now," my mother said, like she'd just happened in on a mountain guest spa, maid included. "I will be spending the night here. I brought an overnight bag just in case." She pointed to a red suitcase in the corner by the front door. She probably imagined herself flowing downstairs in her silk pajamas one button too many undone at the top, after the gang showed up, gin glass in hand, gesturing expansively about something. What? Me and some silly remark I'd made to her earlier.

"A bath," I said. "You still like them real hot?"

"Yes," my mother said. "You don't mind?"

I should have then, maybe, sat down on the sagging double bed Blaire and I were sharing, to weigh all the alternatives one last time before murdering my mother. I should have perhaps considered eternal damnation, sin and the simple fact that even though I wanted her dead, she had given me life and that was a sacred bond, wasn't it? Beyond the earthbound shackles of hate and despair? Weren't you supposed to love your mother no matter what, as the vessel and food of your conception, incubation and birth? So what that she was an evil goddess? She was a goddess, that was a universal given.

I went into the bathroom to run her bath. I poured some aromatic oil, Sensual Dream, into the water and sat on the toilet seat to watch the tub fill. It was a terrible thing I was about to do but it didn't feel terrible. It felt exciting and inevitable. It was something hard that had to be done for the larger good, for the survival of the ecosystem, like deer season or a mastectomy. Would it make me happy? Who knew? I had become a part of a process now, the hot water pouring out of the silver faucet into the clean white tub.

The moral questions out of the way, some questions of aesthetics did remain. The genre of murder, for example. Should it be tastefully Hitchcock, grotesquely DePalma, or bizarre and steely futuristic à la Cameron's *Terminator 2*? Should I speak to her as she struggled under my strong hands, words of enlightenment, scorn or sympathy? And after she died, should there be a ceremony of some sort or nothing at all?

"Your bath's ready"—I called down to her—"anytime you are." And then I headed for the bedroom to wait.

"Come wash my back," she said, a few minutes later. That's when I knew it was almost over. "Use the washcloth. Here's the soap. Nice soap. Did you bring this with you?" She smiled up at me from the water.

I hadn't seen her naked in nearly twenty-five years and she displayed her body proudly, the long flat breasts, the thin brown pubic hair, the pink bunion on her right foot. Would I look like this when I was her age? Could you love someone's body and still hate the rest of them?

I washed her back carefully, memorizing the moles and freckles. She cooed slightly. She was my baby now, she was so much under my touch.

"Wash my chest," she said and, for a moment, I felt excited, as if I'd forgotten she was my mother or I'd remembered she was. I took the blue washcloth and got it soapy and then I began to move it across her chest and breasts. She said, "That's wonderful," and then she pulled me toward her and kissed me deeply on the mouth. I kissed her back. My first lover, my permanent compulsion, my two-headed demon.

"I love you," I said and then I pushed her chest and head under the water. She didn't resist at all. I wondered if she thought we were playing a game or doing water ballet. She just slid down the curve of the tub smooth. Then her legs began to kick so I climbed in the tub and sat on her stomach with my hands on her shoulders to keep her down. She tried to pull me off with her thighs and she was strong, much stronger than I could believe. She wanted to live. I looked at her face. I looked into her eyes. They were open wide under the water and they were watching me.

"Good-bye," I said and stared at her face to see what would happen next. But there was nothing in her eyes, not recognition, not fear, not peace, not anger, not forgiveness. I reached one arm behind me to hold down her legs and one of her arms flew up to grab at me.

At first, I looked at her arm, without passion, as if it were a kinetic work of sculpture but soon an unpleasant sensation came over me. I began to feel like I was looking at my own arm, sinewy and freckled, sprinkled lightly with blond hairs. My mother and I looked alike and so did our arms.

I pulled on it and stood up, pulling her with me.

She coughed and bent over to catch her breath in big gasps of air. Then she stood up and slapped me hard across the face.

"You tried to kill me again, didn't you?" she shouted at me. We were standing up in the bathtub, me in dripping jeans and sneakers and T-shirt and my mother naked. "Why'd you stop?"

She climbed out and put a towel around her. She didn't seem afraid of me at all.

"Why'd you stop?" she said, quieter this time. "You're a freak and a coward," she said. "You know that? You're a sicko, a nothing."

Her mouth got tight and she stared at me with such rage I thought she might slap me again. But she didn't. She just stood there and looked wet and gray and shriveled.

"Why did you stop?" she said. "Answer me, goddamn it. Answer me that it's because, compared to me, you don't matter. You're nobody. You do not matter in this world." And then she walked out of the room to go get her clothes. She walked right past me because she wasn't afraid of me and because she wasn't even grateful that I'd saved her life.

It was her fucking arm that stopped me, of course.

She was not dead because I didn't want to spend the rest of my life looking at my arm and thinking about hers.

While I packed to leave I pretended I had killed her, for the hell of it, just to think about what I would have done next.

I'd have had to tell Blaire about it and then I'd get to watch her squirm. She'd have to know it was partly her own fault for telling my mother where we were and then leaving us in the house alone.

Then we'd dig a hole and bury her in the backyard.

I'd have to tell Doris and Tina to get rid of the car. They'd be so pissed at me for dragging them in as accomplices, they'd never speak to me again. Except that first Doris would make some remark about me not being God and Tina would beg to go home.

In spite of everything, it was probably good I didn't kill my mother.

And the best part about it was that, this time, I didn't just fail. I pulled her out of the water because that was exactly what I wanted to do.

I didn't write Blaire a note or anything. I decided that if she wanted to, she could figure out where I'd gone.

39

Where I was going was back to El Encanto in Taos, the place it all began. I'm not speaking literally. Life's such a goddamn continuum, hardly anything is ever literal. I'm speaking of my love affair with Blaire and my second flirtation with murder.

I got to the big gate at dinnertime the next night. When I pressed the intercom button Sister Dorothy answered me right away.

"You're all alone?" she said. "You drove all that way?" I hadn't called her from the road or asked permission to stay. I wasn't that organized in my mind.

"You're all alone too?" I said. "In that big house? Aren't you scared?"

"Nobody telephoned looking for you," she said. "In case you're doing this as some sort of gesture."

"Oh, Sister," I said, "will you let me in even though I'm a terrible sinner?"

And the gates to heaven swung open, just like that.

"Now what?" Sister Dorothy said, greeting me at the door. "You hungry?"

She looked exactly the same—habit, veil, rosary beads. I noticed her face more this time though, probably because there were just the two of us. It was round and unlined, girlish almost, with smart blue eyes.

"I'd like to make a donation to the order, if you'll let me," I said. "For staying here. I'd like to spend the night."

"This isn't a retreat house," she said, leading me inside. "But maybe it's a good idea to open one, come to think of it. Maybe there's lots more like you out there. Could that be possible?"

While I wanted to encourage Dorothy's entrepreneurial spirit, I rather hoped not. I hoped everybody else could get most of the good stuff they needed without having to go so far from home.

"I have this tendency to externalize everything," I said. "Good mother, bad mother, you know what I mean. I don't have enough going on by myself."

"This isn't a therapy group," Sister Dorothy said, ignoring me. "All I have is eggs, milk and bread." She was taking me into the kitchen so I could get something to eat.

"I know," I said. "I won't do it again."

She pointed to the refrigerator. "Food's in there," she said. "I'll leave your bedroom door open. Sheets and towels on the bed. Okay with you?"

"Swell," I said.

She smiled at me and left to work on marketing strategies for the new retreat center. She told me I was a blessing in disguise.

It was 7:30 P.M. and I was about to be a new person. I was at a retreat house about to grapple in solitary with my psyche.

Except that there was a telephone on the counter next to the stove. I could still try to call Blaire.

My last poem

Still Life of a Woman

When they found me I was staring
Sideways like a dead fish
Lying flat on a long wooden table in the
Kitchen.
In my hand a stainless steel carving knife

Caught the light on its blade and
Scattered it like silver fish scales
Across my naked body.
I wasn't dead, exactly.
I was waiting for the resurrection.
Someone to take the knife and murder me
And then breathe me back to life
Or, barring that, fillet me
And feed me to the guests.

I didn't know what should happen next so, to buy time, I made myself a fried egg sandwich and ate it with a glass of milk. Then I paced off the 135 alternating gray and pink linoleum squares on the floor, 93 times. I counted Dorothy's flatware and arranged it so the tines, serrated edges and concave surfaces all faced the same way. I drank a couple gallons of water and ate several spoonfuls of salt. I pulled out a circle of hair from the crown of my head. I held my breath for 2 minutes and 35 seconds and then I did 225 sit-ups.

I wanted to call Blaire so I'd know the worst, like if she was lovers with my mother now or what. And if I knew the worst, I'd also know the best, like maybe she wasn't, and she was going to come here and make me forgive her again.

"This is obviously the downside of opening a retreat center," Sister Dorothy said, when she came back. "People having nervous breakdowns in the kitchen." It was about eleven o'clock and she was dressed for bed in a simple white flannel nightgown. Her gray-blond hair was curling girlishly around her shoulders.

"You have hair," I said. "Don't you have to cut it off?"

"No," she said. "I call the shots now. That's the upside of running your own order."

"So what's the secret, Sister?" I said.

"You been eating salt?" she said. She was sitting on a stool fiddling with the saltcellar I'd been using.

'Yeah," I said. "Only a little bit."

"The secret is . . . ," she said. "Let's see."

"I'm drinking water too," I said to show her I wasn't completely nuts.

"I like secrets," she said. "But I have to think about it a minute."

While she thought about it, I pulled out another clump of hair.

"Don't do that," Dorothy said. "Oh, go ahead, do it. You need to do it, do it. What the heck."

And then, because she was dressed like a normal woman now, I realized that Sister Dorothy was probably just about my age. I'd been thinking of her as much older because of the habit, but looking at her soft, full face, I thought that maybe she was even younger than me.

And I wondered why in hell I was asking a nun, unlined from avoiding human affairs her entire lifetime, about what the secret to life was.

"Okay," she said. "I think I've got it."

"What?" I said.

"In the long run, doing the hard thing is easier."

"What's that mean?" I said, as if I was going to really use her advice. "It sounds pretty Catholic."

"You're on the right track already. You just don't know it," she said, this time sounding more like a cryptic fortune cookie.

At about 12:30 I decided I wanted Blaire to come to El Encanto to try to get me back so I could have the pleasure of rejecting her.

And that's as far as I got that night.

My dream

In my dream, I was about to give birth to a litter of puppies. The father was a German shepherd and the mother was a Welsh Corgi but I was the designated place of incubation. My stomach hurt because the puppies inside me had sharp nails and I was annoyed by all the sniffing attention I was getting from canine parents and friends in the delivery room. I called out to Sister Dorothy, evidently nurse in charge, to get the room cleared, that I was about to deliver. And then the best part happened. It was so cool. The puppies came out, their parents returned and cleaned them off. When I woke up I was so happy!

40

The next day, Sister Dorothy drove me up into the mountains, a service she made clear wasn't going to be part of the regular retreat package. We sat down on the edge of a cliff so we could swing our feet and look out over the valley. The sky was bright blue and the land below us was mostly brown and flat except for small deposits of snow and ribbons of water running on the ground. It was so beautiful and quiet that I actually felt like myself for the first time in years. In a lifetime, maybe.

We didn't talk too much but when we did, Sister Dorothy would say something like, "Have you noticed how everything ends up with murder these days?"

And I'd think she meant something about me until she said, "Art, music, fiction, even sports. Somebody gets killed, or just misses getting killed, or remembers an important murder in the past."

"How do you know that?" I'd say. "Aren't you cloistered?"

"I get cable," she said. "I get the Sunday *Times*. I'm not saying it's wrong. I'm just making an observation."

"You mean something happened to natural causes," I said, "as a structural device?"

"Bingo," she said.

"I started seeing Blaire Bennett after the workshop," I said. "The poet who taught here."

"Oh," Sister Dorothy said. "She's famous, isn't she?"

"Yeah," I said. "Who needs it? Then, a couple days ago, I almost killed my mother."

"Women," she said.

We were quiet for a while and I thought that it was sort of like being with Doris, sitting here with Dorothy. It was easier though because I had less to lose, the two of us not being quite friends yet.

"Have you ever loved a woman?" I said. "I mean besides the Virgin?"

"Eat a sandwich," she said. "Here." And she handed me an egg salad on whole wheat that she'd made back at El Encanto. It was fabulous. Just the right amount of mustard, mayo and onion, smashed but not pasty. Egg salad had probably been a popular dish back in the old days when there was a real convent.

"Listen, Dorothy," I said, finally. "All I want to know is, if the only morality is in our own heads how do we make a good decision, murder or otherwise? I mean, everything can't be natural causes."

She turned toward me, put her hand on my cheek and kissed me lightly on the lips. There was a little bit of starched coif involved but mostly it was a very nice thing.

"You sound so young," she said. "You sound like a little girl. Such innocence, such trust. You ought to join my order before the world eats you up."

But Blaire was waiting at El Encanto when we got back.

She was sitting on a chair by a window in the main hall, all in black except for a big silver buckle on her belt. The first feeling I had was this extreme gratefulness that I was important enough for her to come here to see. Then I had this feeling of fear because of all the pain she had come to deliver. Then I felt this rage because she wasn't loving me right, the way I deserved.

"What's up?" she said, too cool. She was hiding something and she was so dumb she thought I wouldn't notice.

"You told my mother where we'd be," I said. "You didn't consult me. You went for a long walk with her in the woods knowing it would drive me crazy. Then you left me all alone with her in the cabin with knives and poison."

"And bathtubs," Blaire said. She stood up and came over to me. She put her hands on my shoulders. I twisted away from her which I could tell was a big surprise.

"You knew I had it in me," I said. "You were behind the whole thing. You wrote the script."

Blaire ran her hand through her spiky white hair as if she was having trouble following the things I had to say. While I watched her I felt sad because I realized I would never make love with her again. And I felt sad because she didn't know it yet.

"Forgive me, darling," she said, reaching for my hand. I let her take it. I looked into her eyes and what I saw reflected in them wasn't my face at all.

"You slept with my mother, didn't you?" I said. She took her hand away and walked back to her chair. I'd known she'd done it from the moment I first saw her but hearing the words out loud made it hurt worse. What was left of my heart closed in on itself in a tight little fist.

"What can I say?" she said, like she was the casualty instead of me. "You and your mother. You two spun me like a top. I carried messages between you like a hungry pigeon. Do you know that? You and your mother are the lovers. I'm the stuntwoman. I'm not even in real life."

I could see that she was crying and that it was my turn to ask her to forgive me. But I couldn't find much to go on in what she'd just said. She'd probably thought it up two minutes ago but she already believed the hell out of it. That was the thing.

It would have sounded terrific in that marble hall if I'd yelled swear words at her or thrown something that crashed into pieces but I wasn't in the mood. I wasn't in the mood for murder and I wasn't in the mood for Blaire.

I was in the mood for being the first one out the door for a change.

So I ran upstairs and packed my things. I wrote Dorothy a note, stuck several twenties in the card to cover spending the night and propped it up on the dresser. Then I went downstairs and walked over to tell Blaire good-bye.

"I'm leaving," I said.

"But I drove all this way," she said.

"Oh well," I said.

"You're not leaving me," Blaire said. "I've invested too much."

That's when I remembered I was supposed to thank her for all the things I'd learned from knowing her.

"And thanks," I said, "for helping me feel valuable." It was corny but so what, it was true. Then I said, "I don't think I'll be writing any more poetry, though. It isn't exactly me."